S0-EJI-997

I Like to Read® Comics instill confidence and the joy of reading in new readers. Created by award-winning artists as well as talented newcomers, these imaginative books support beginners' reading comprehension with extensive visual support.

We want to hear every new reader say, "I like to read comics!"

Visit our website for flash cards, activities, and more about the series:
www.holidayhouse.com/ILiketoRead
#ILTR

To JaJaMaKa—Jade, Martina, and Katie

Text and illustrations copyright © 2023 by Jannie Ho
All Rights Reserved
HOLIDAY HOUSE is registered in the U.S. Patent and Trademark Office.
Printed and bound in July 2023 at C&C Offset, Shenzhen, China.
The artwork was created in Procreate.
www.holidayhouse.com
First Edition
1 3 5 7 9 10 8 6 4 2

Library of Congress Cataloging-in-Publication Data is available.
ISBN: 978-0-8234-5315-3 (hardcover)

The Lost MITTEN

Jannie Ho

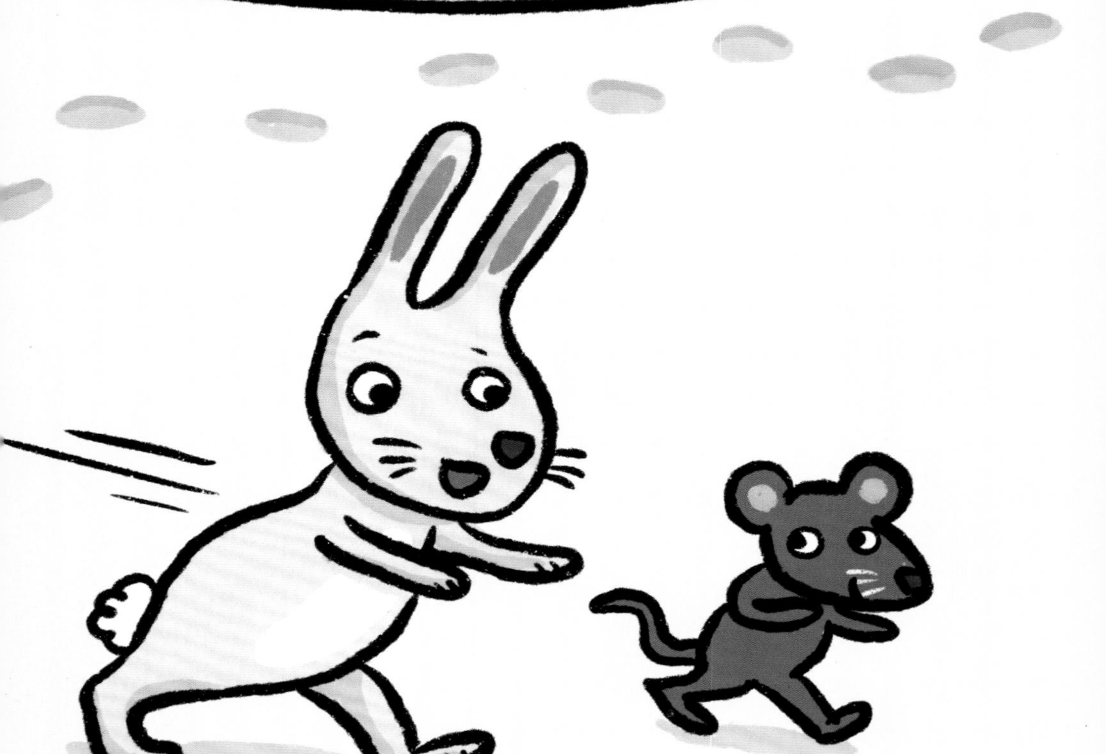

I Like to Read® COMICS™

HOLIDAY HOUSE • NEW YORK

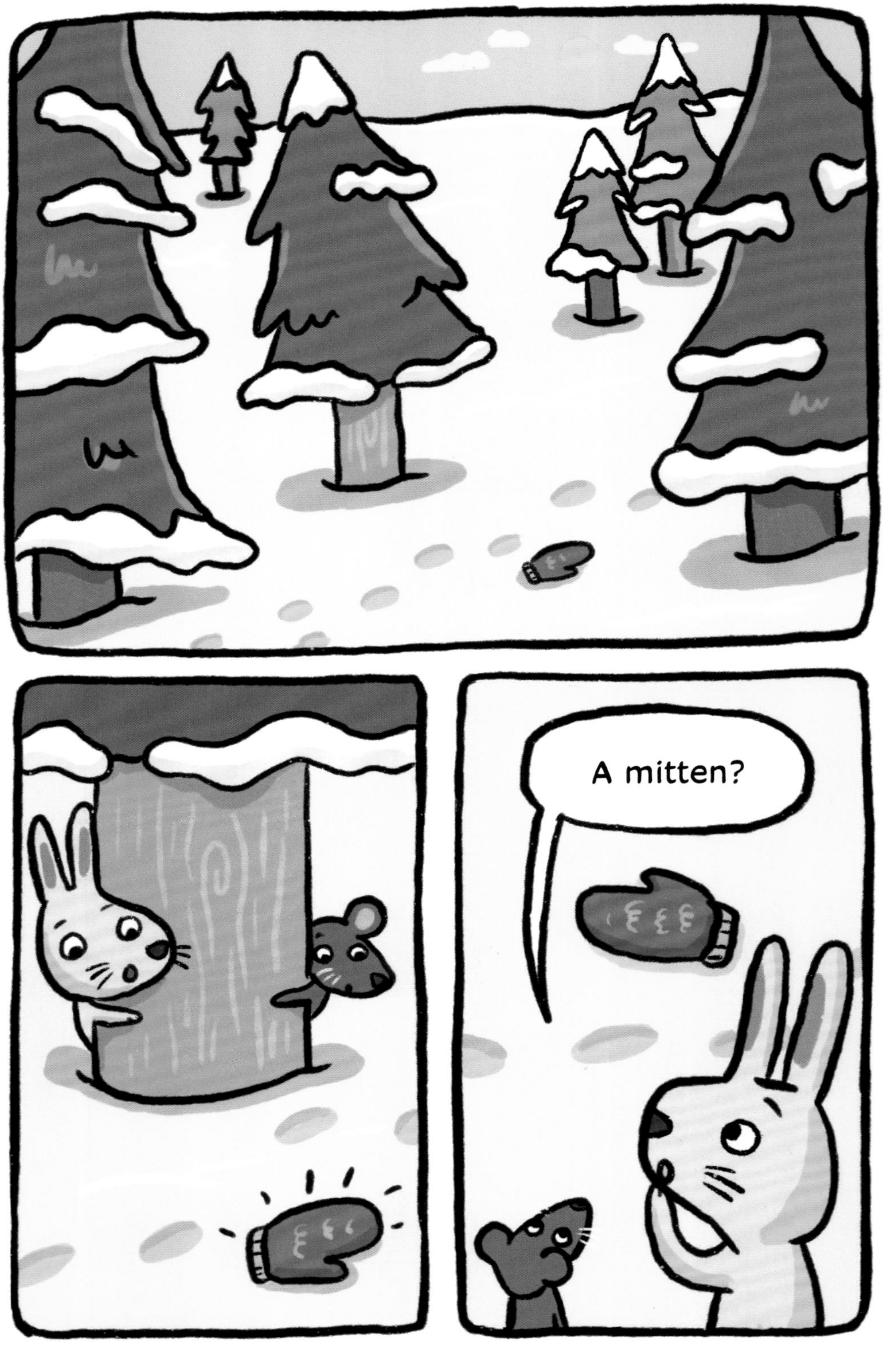
A mitten?

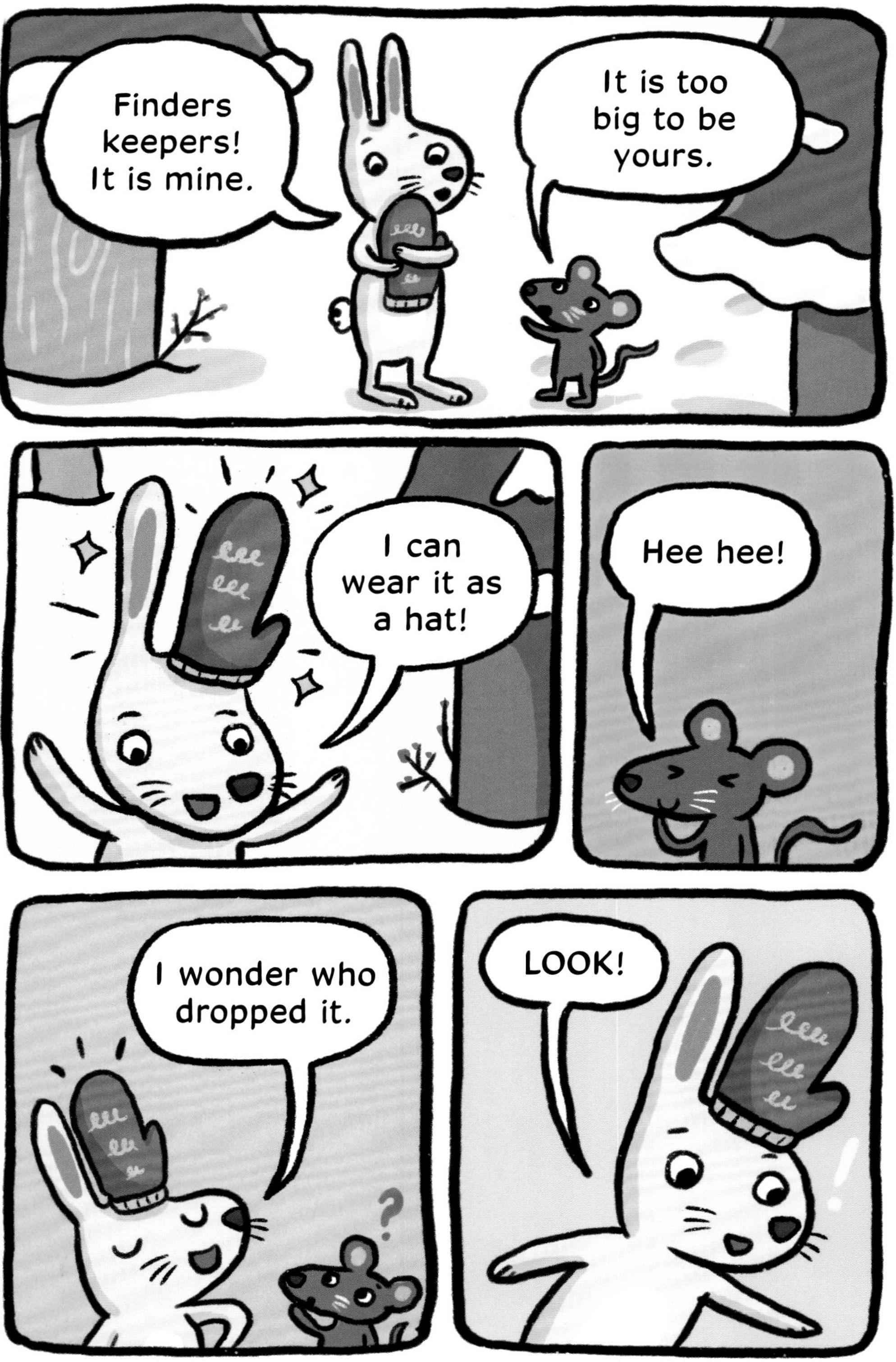
Finders keepers! It is mine.
It is too big to be yours.
I can wear it as a hat!
Hee hee!
I wonder who dropped it.
LOOK!

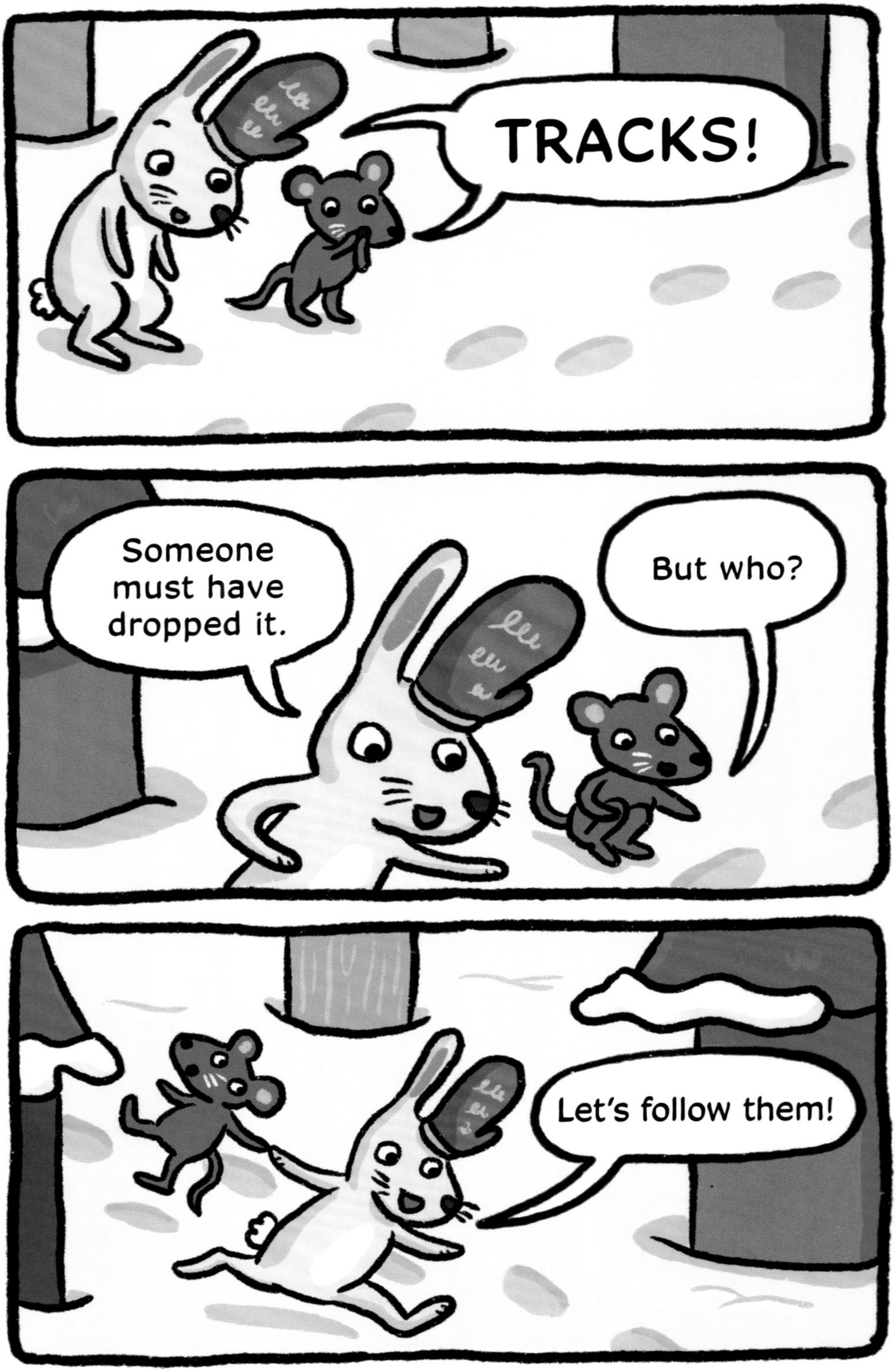
TRACKS!
Someone must have dropped it.
But who?
Let's follow them!

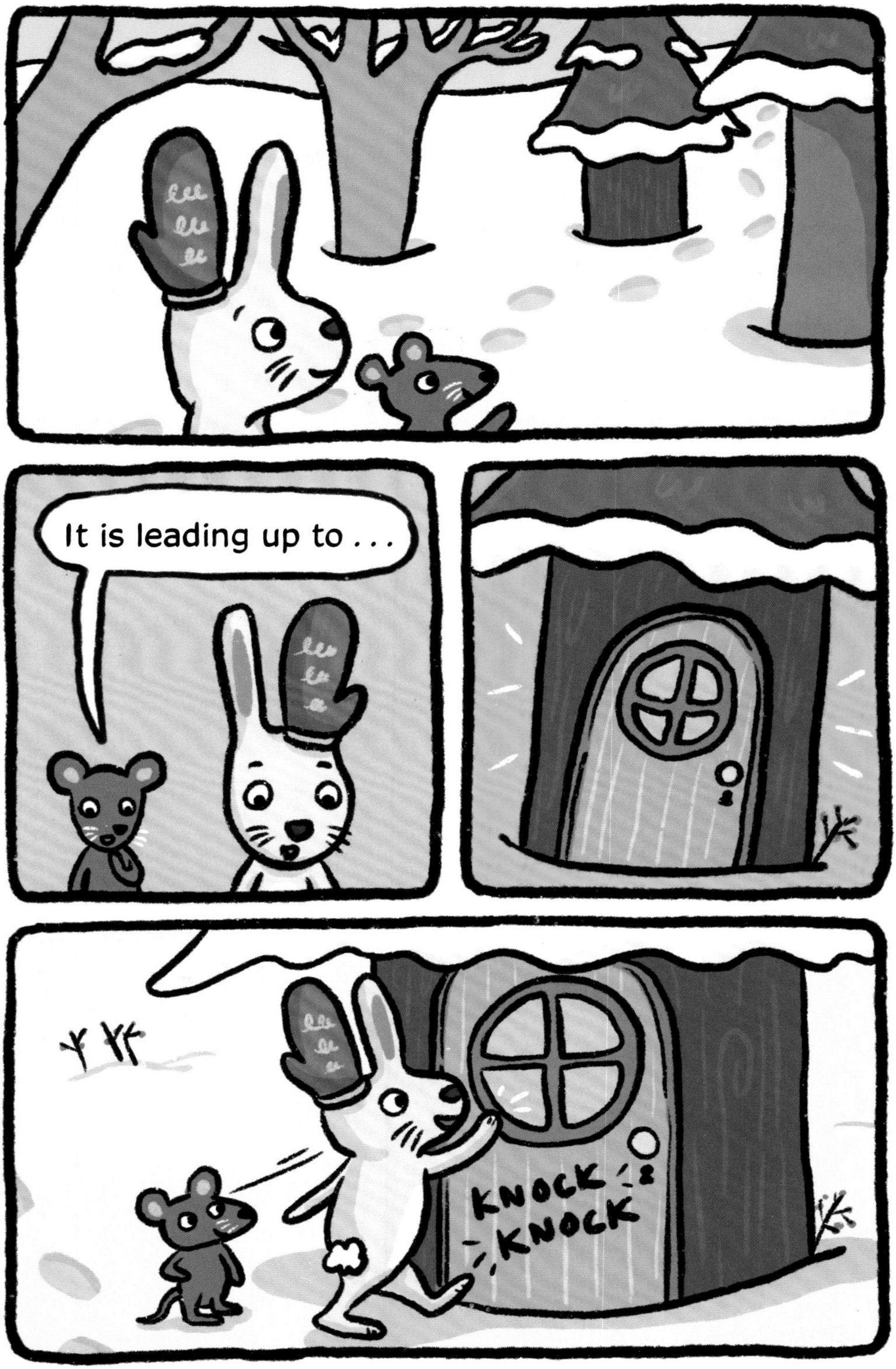
It is leading up to . . .
KNOCK
KNOCK

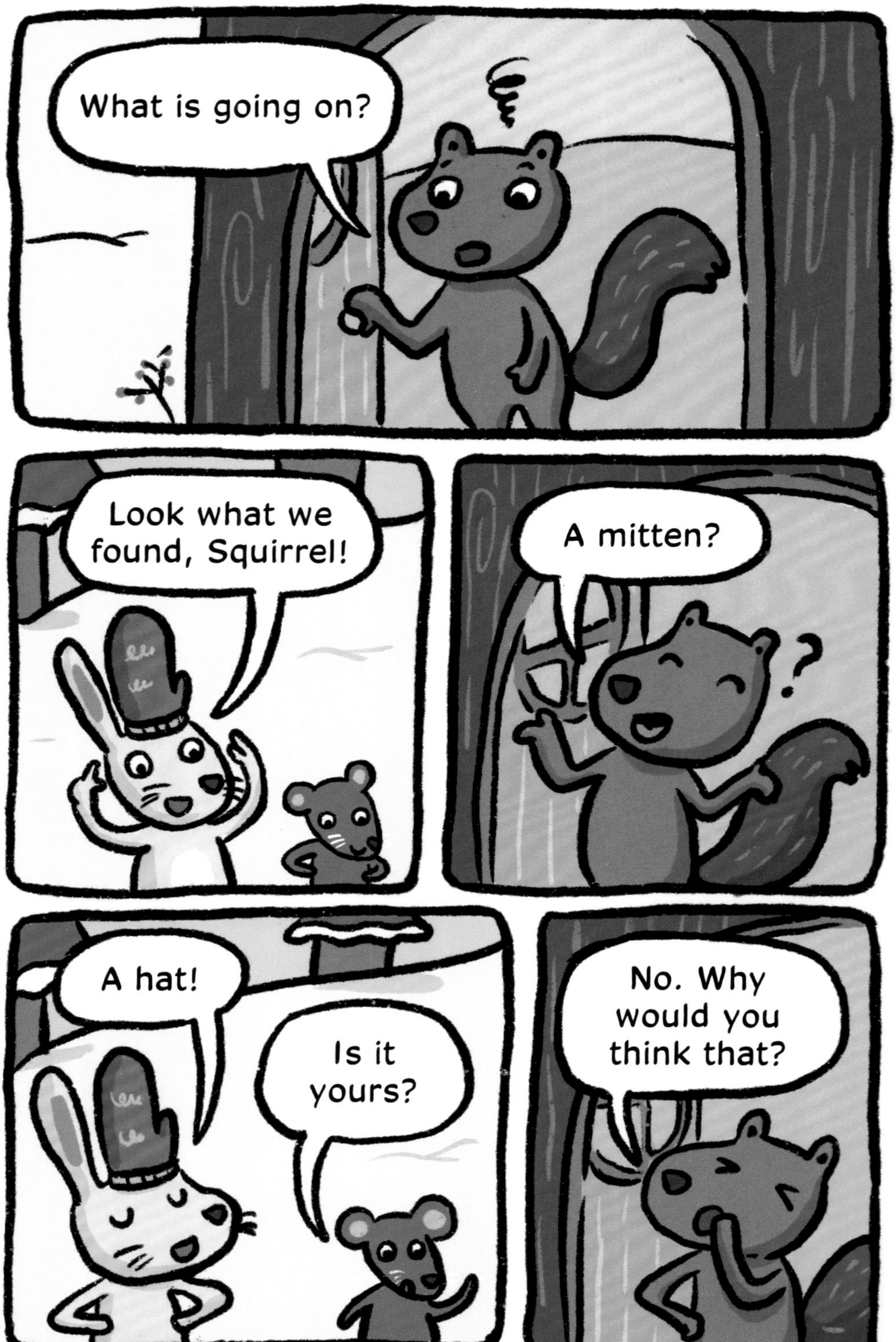
What is going on?
Look what we found, Squirrel!
A mitten?
A hat!
Is it yours?
No. Why would you think that?

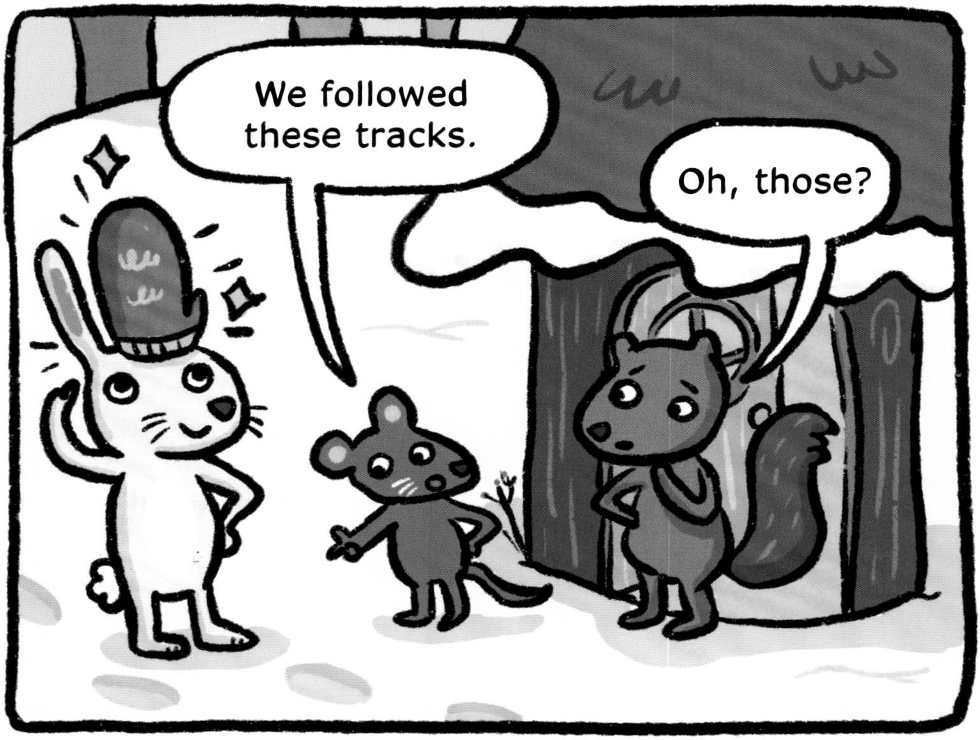
We followed these tracks.
Oh, those?
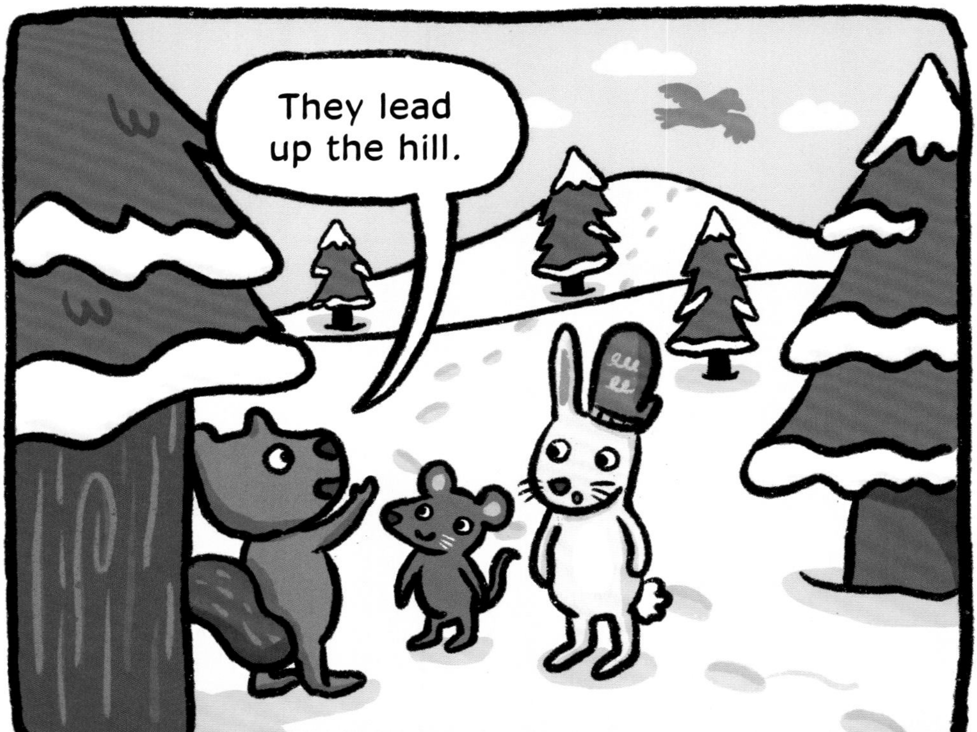
They lead up the hill.

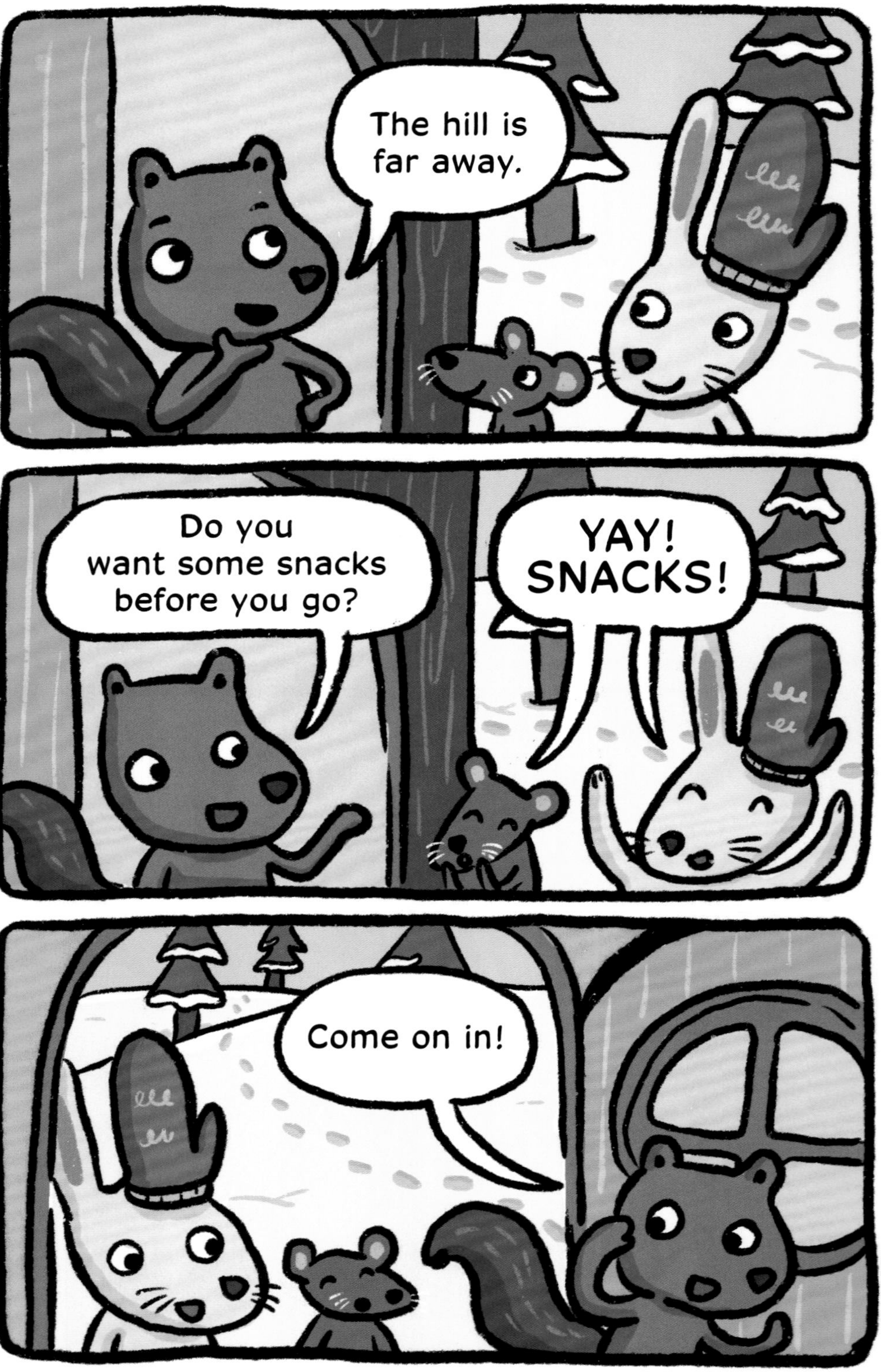
The hill is far away.
Do you want some snacks before you go?
YAY! SNACKS!
Come on in!

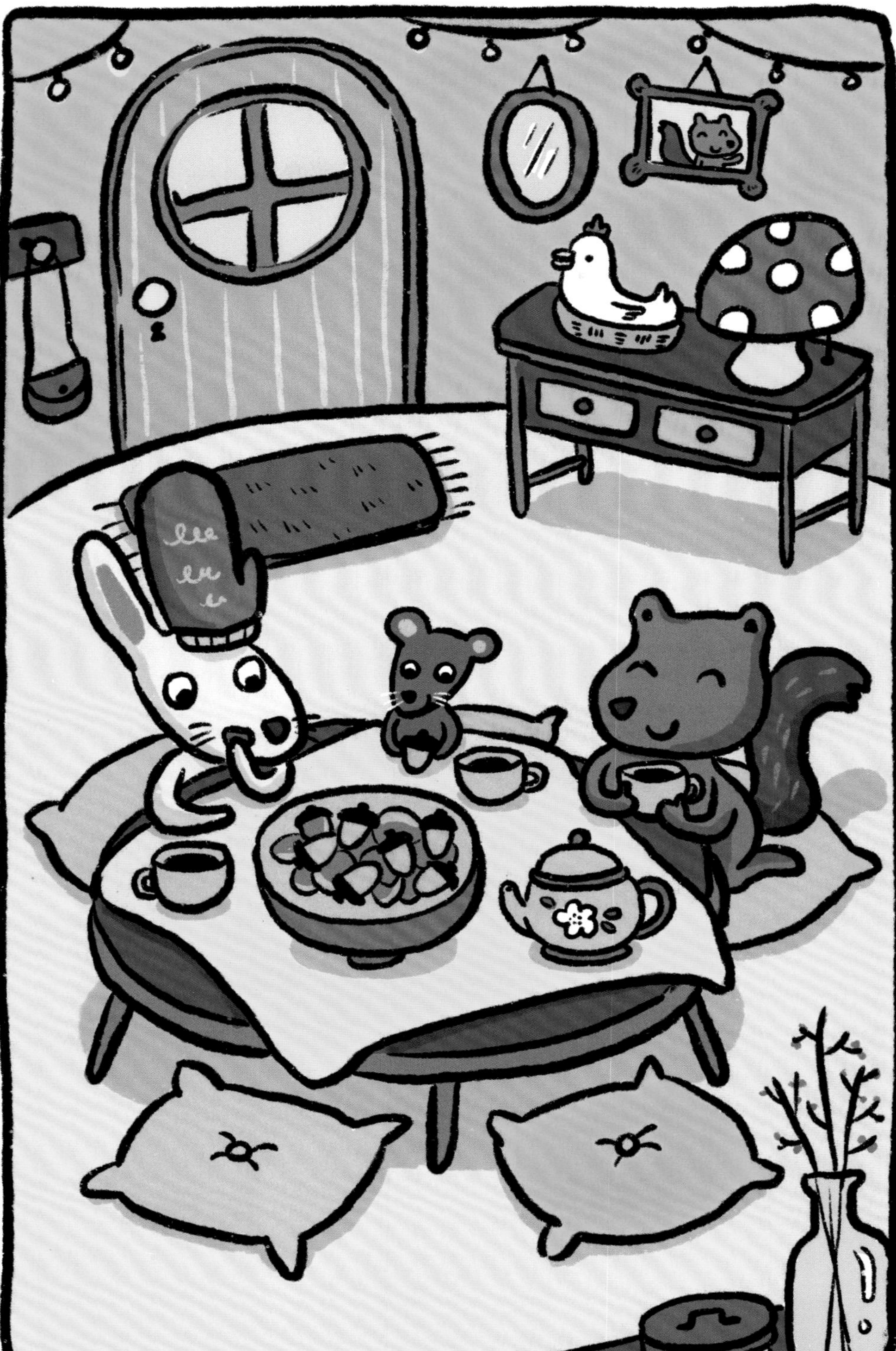

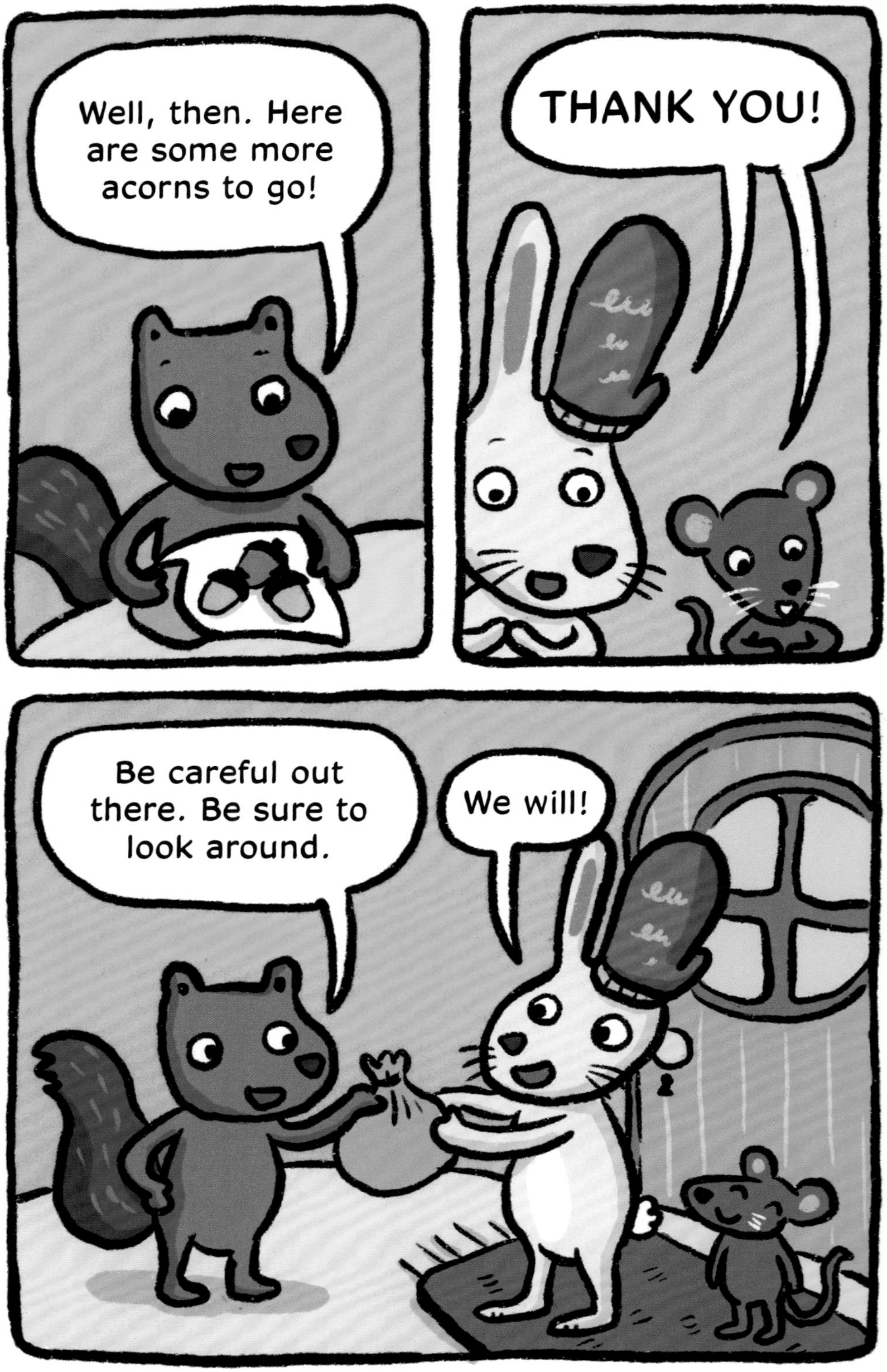
Well, then. Here are some more acorns to go!
THANK YOU!
Be careful out there. Be sure to look around.
We will!

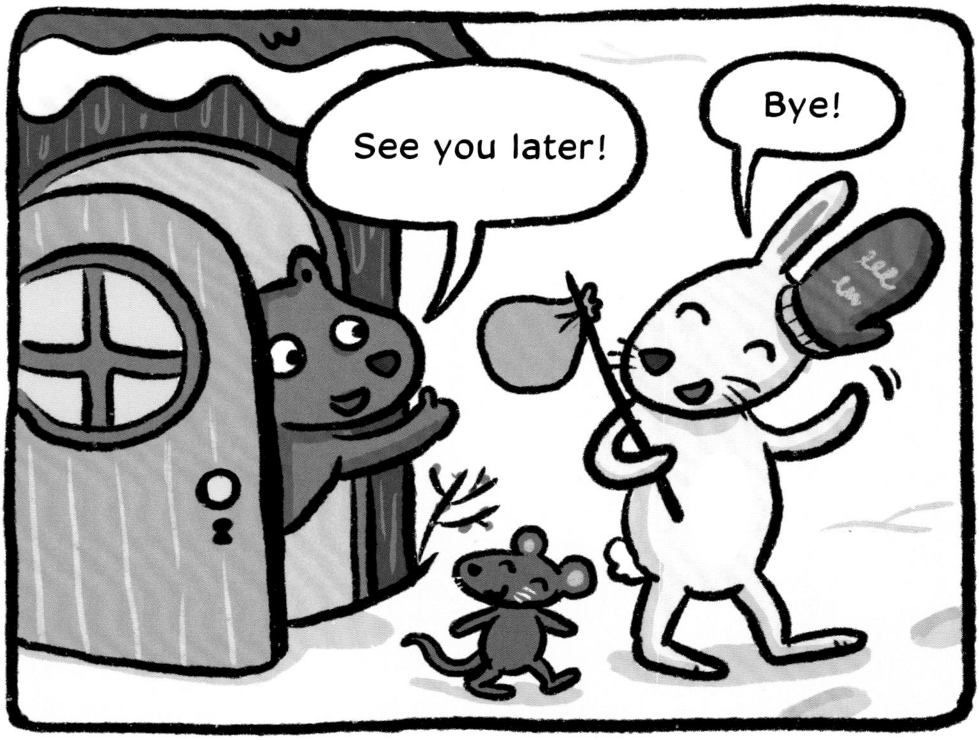
See you later!
Bye!

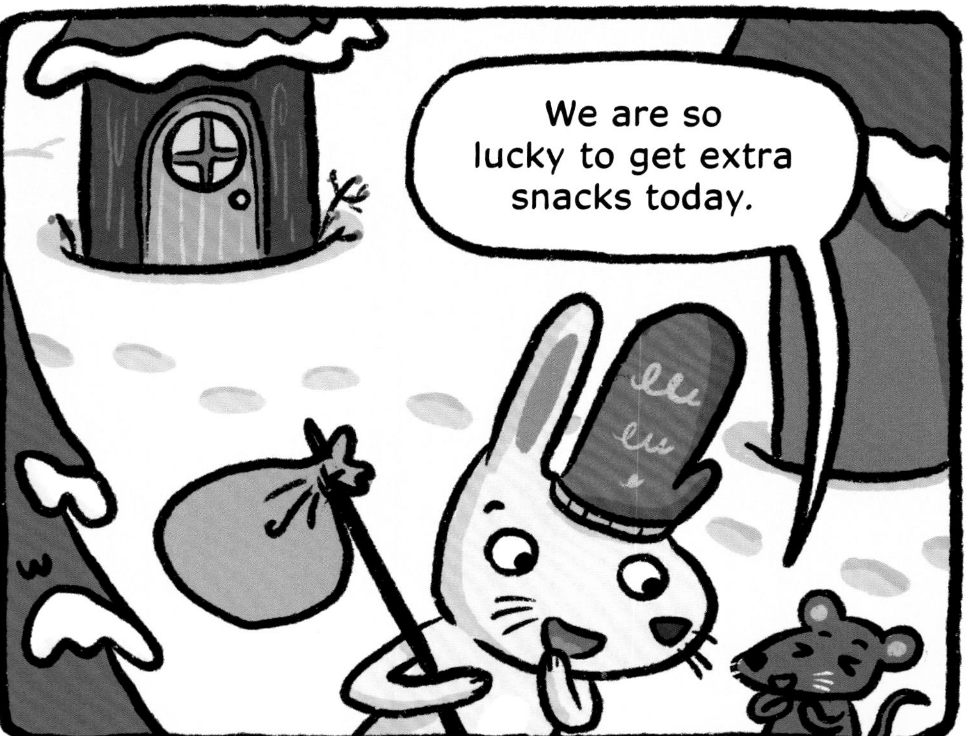
We are so lucky to get extra snacks today.

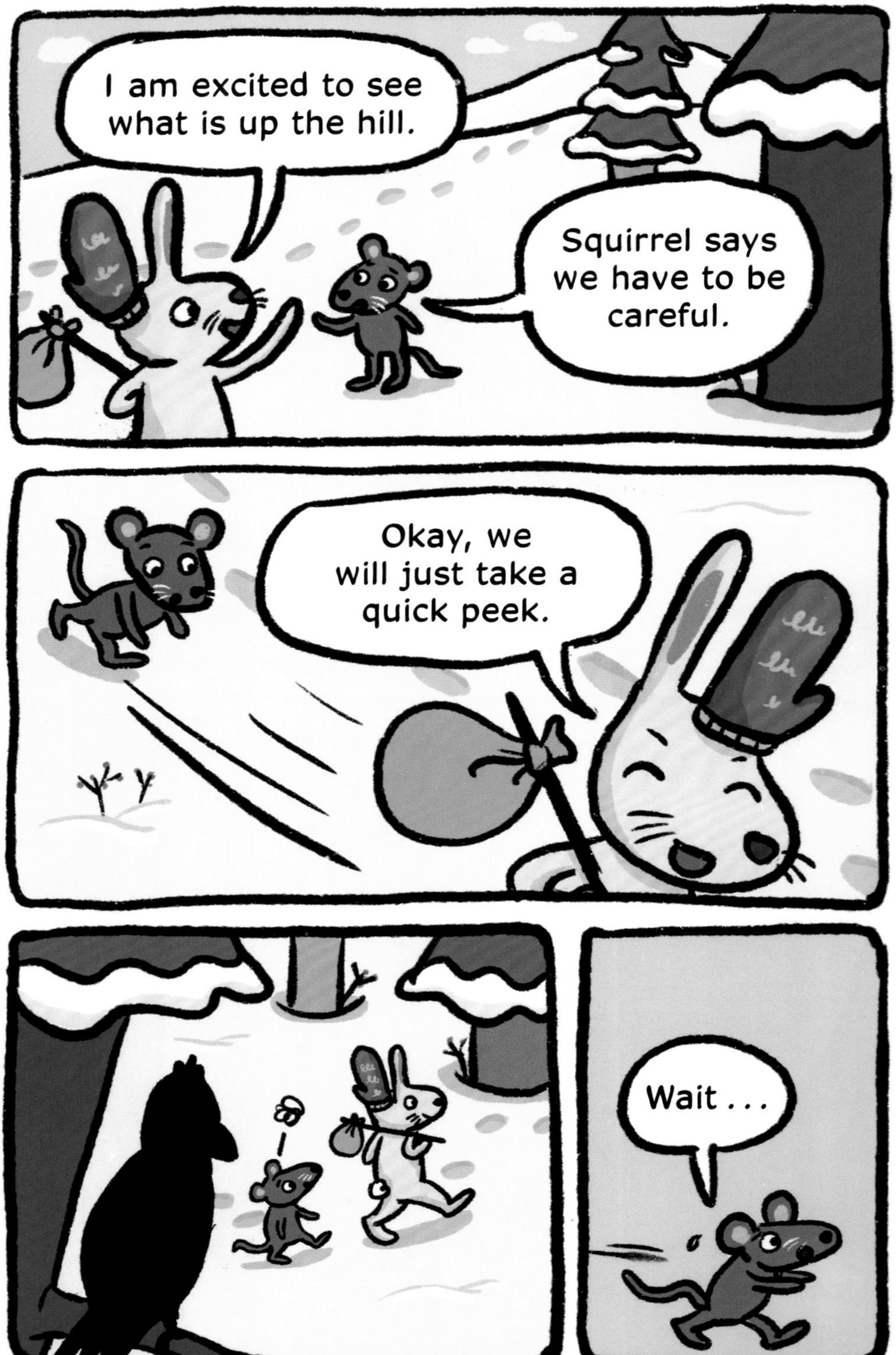
I am excited to see what is up the hill.
Squirrel says we have to be careful.
Okay, we will just take a quick peek.
Wait . . .

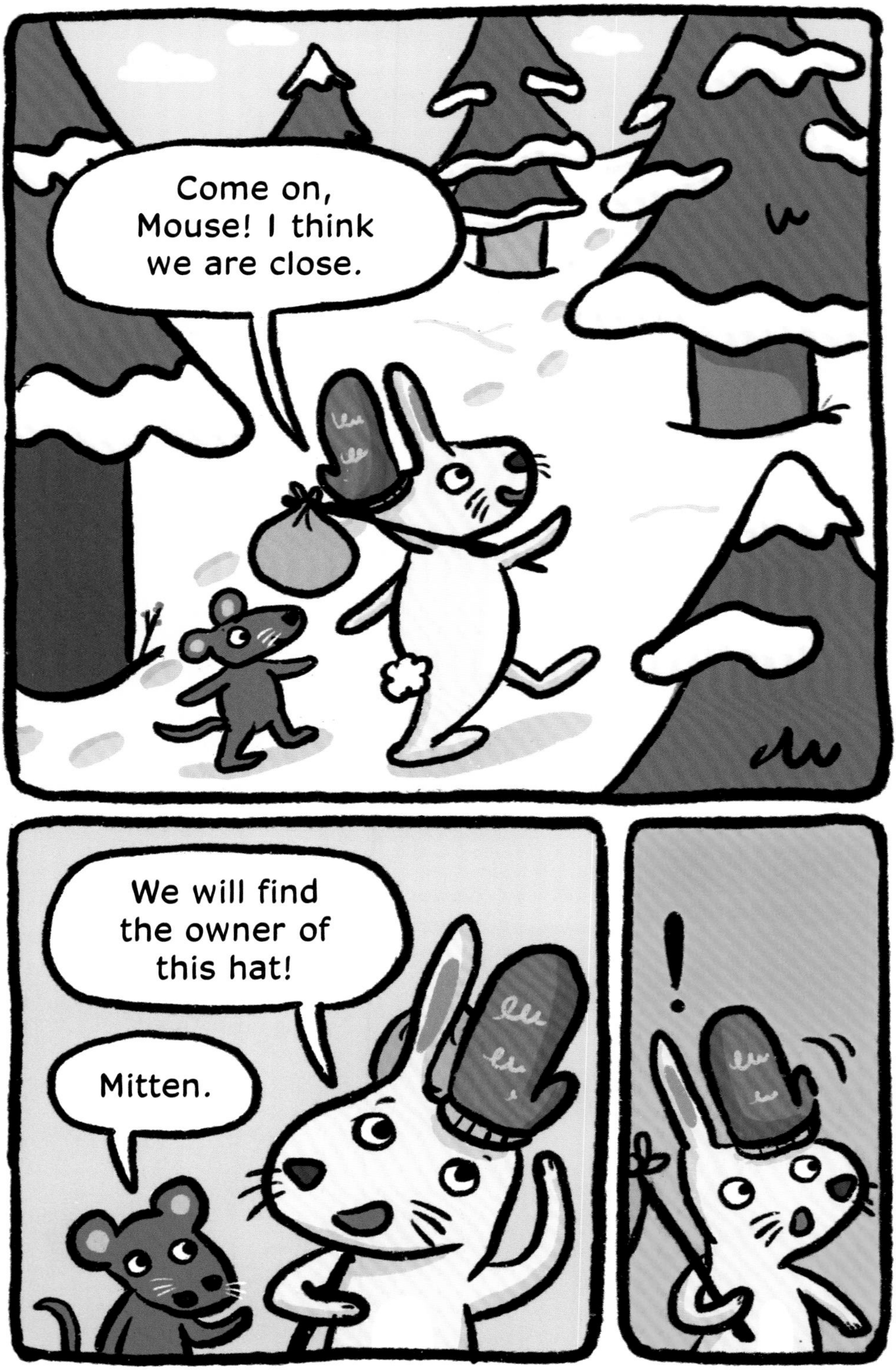
Come on, Mouse! I think we are close.
We will find the owner of this hat!
Mitten.
!

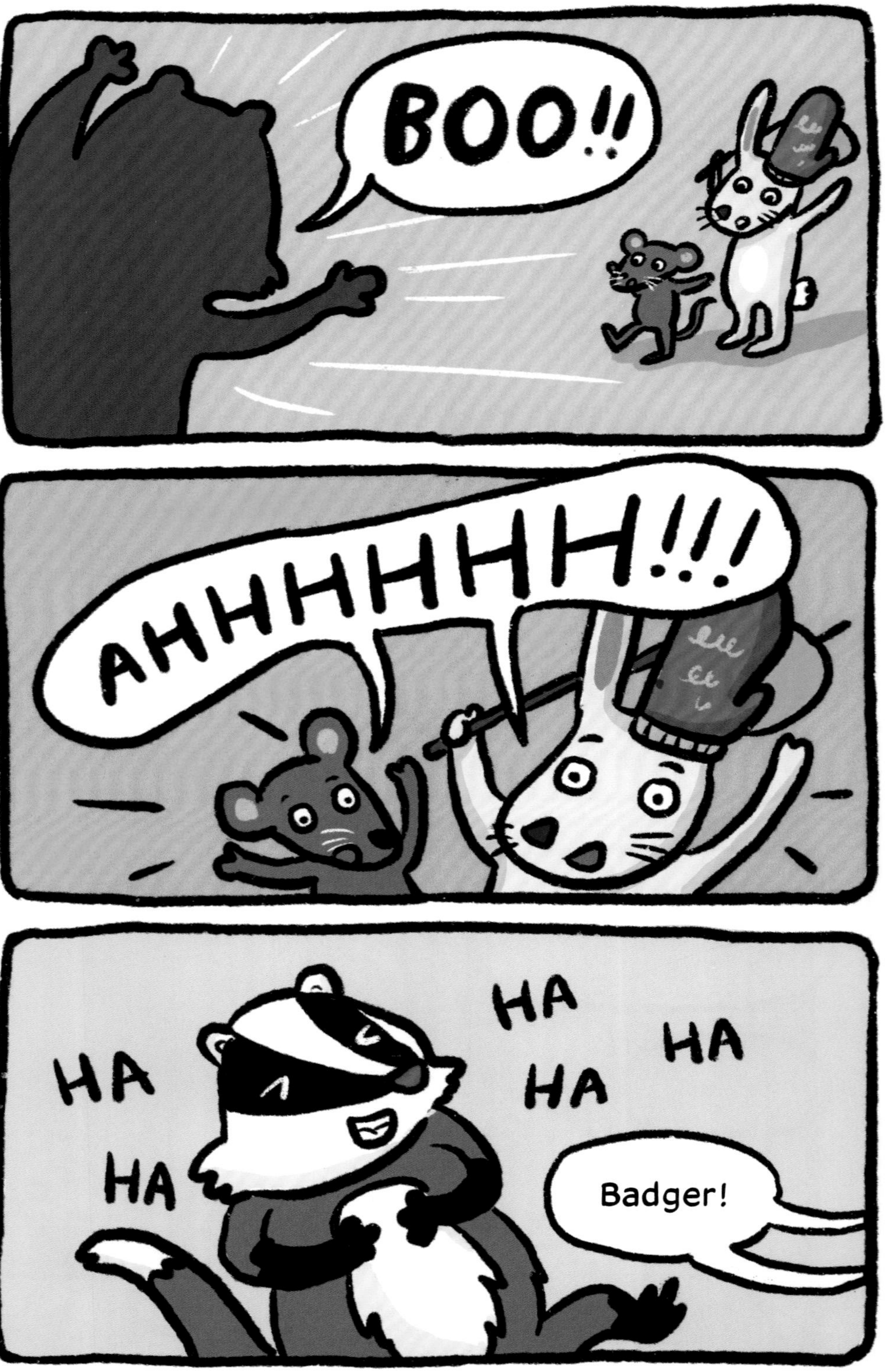
BOO!!
AHHHHHHH!!!
HA
HA
HA
HA
HA
Badger!

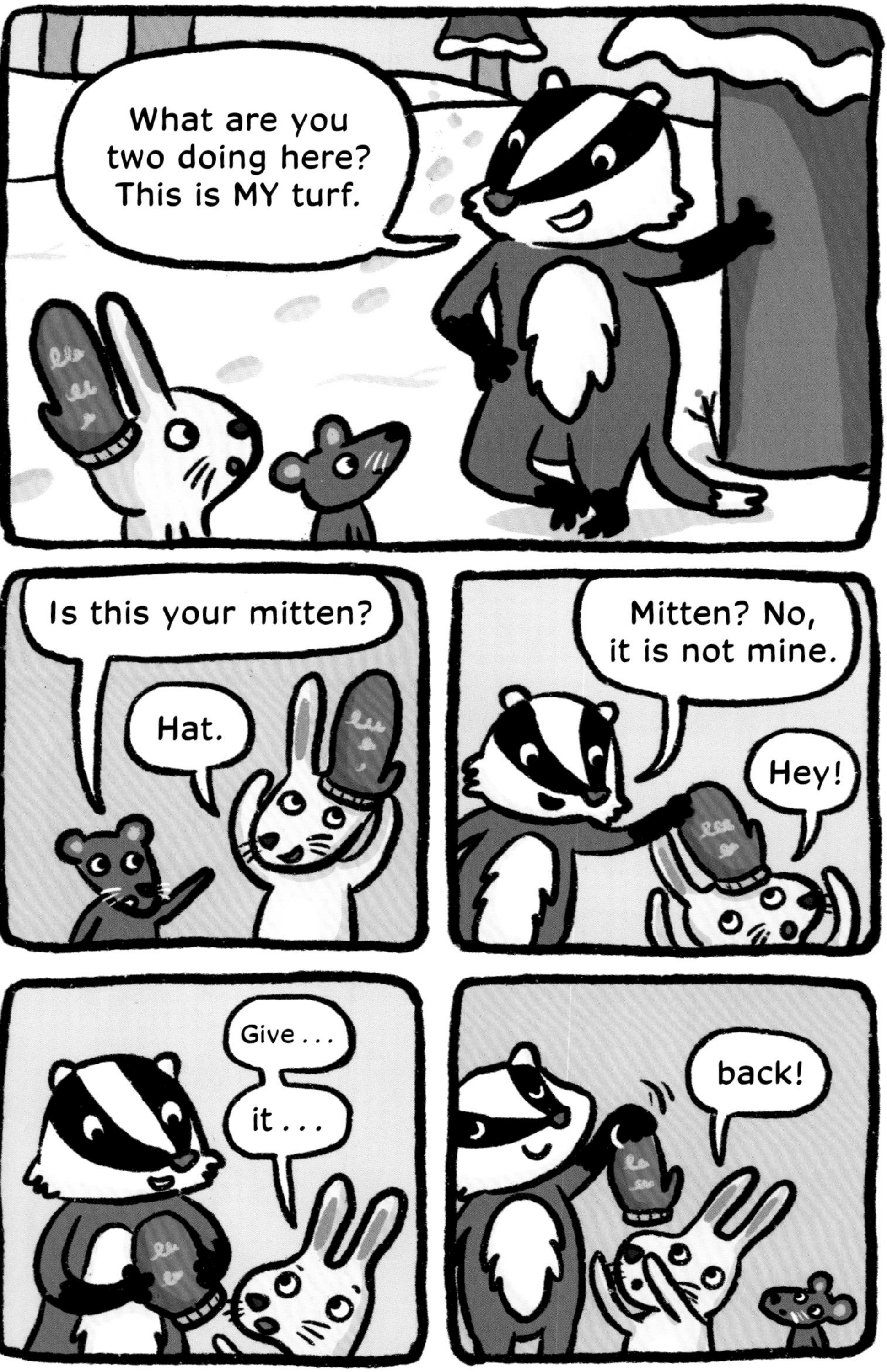
What are you two doing here? This is MY turf.
Is this your mitten?
Hat.
Mitten? No, it is not mine.
Hey!
Give . . .
it . . .
back!

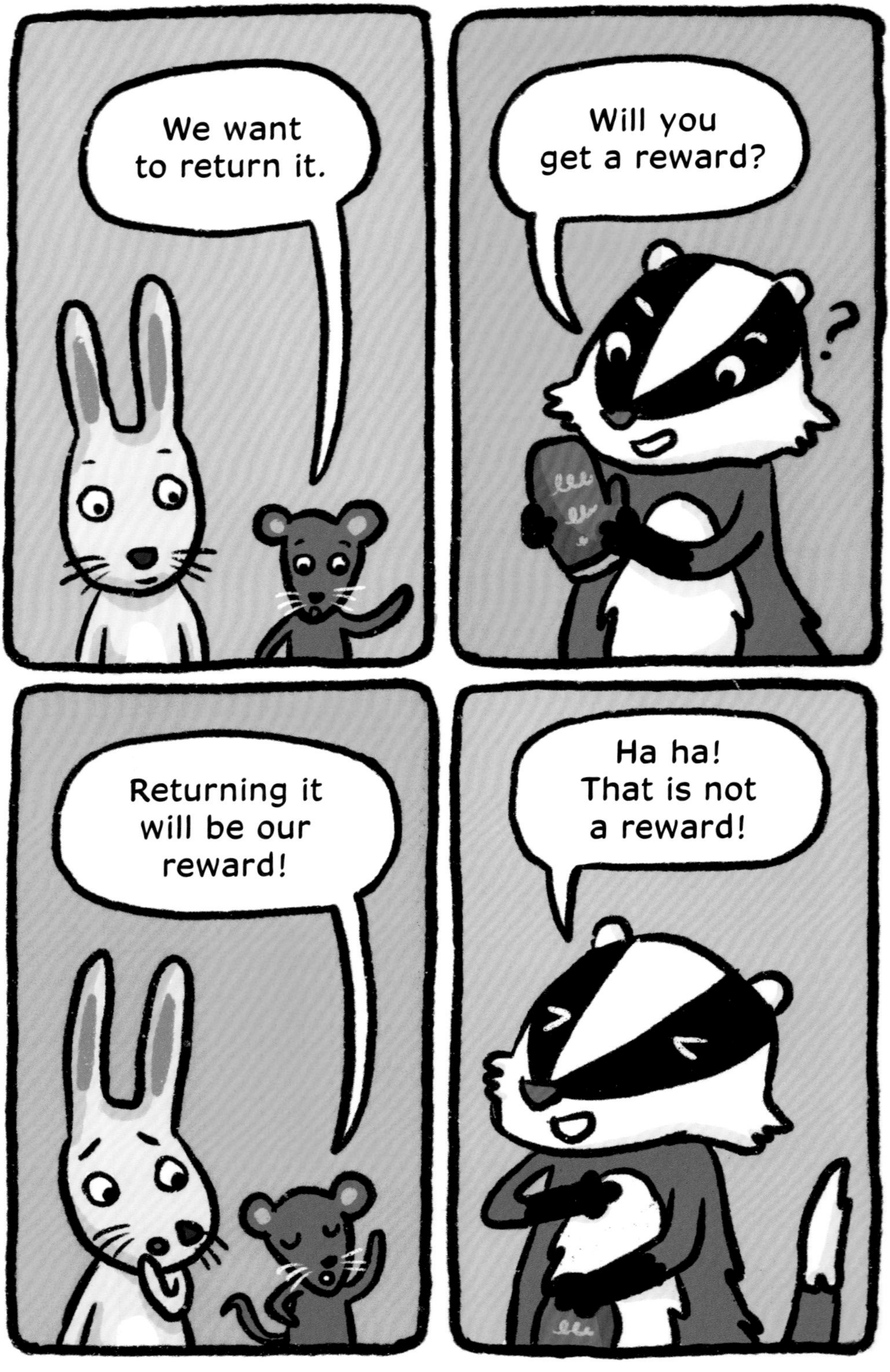
We want to return it.
Will you get a reward?
Returning it will be our reward!
Ha ha! That is not a reward!

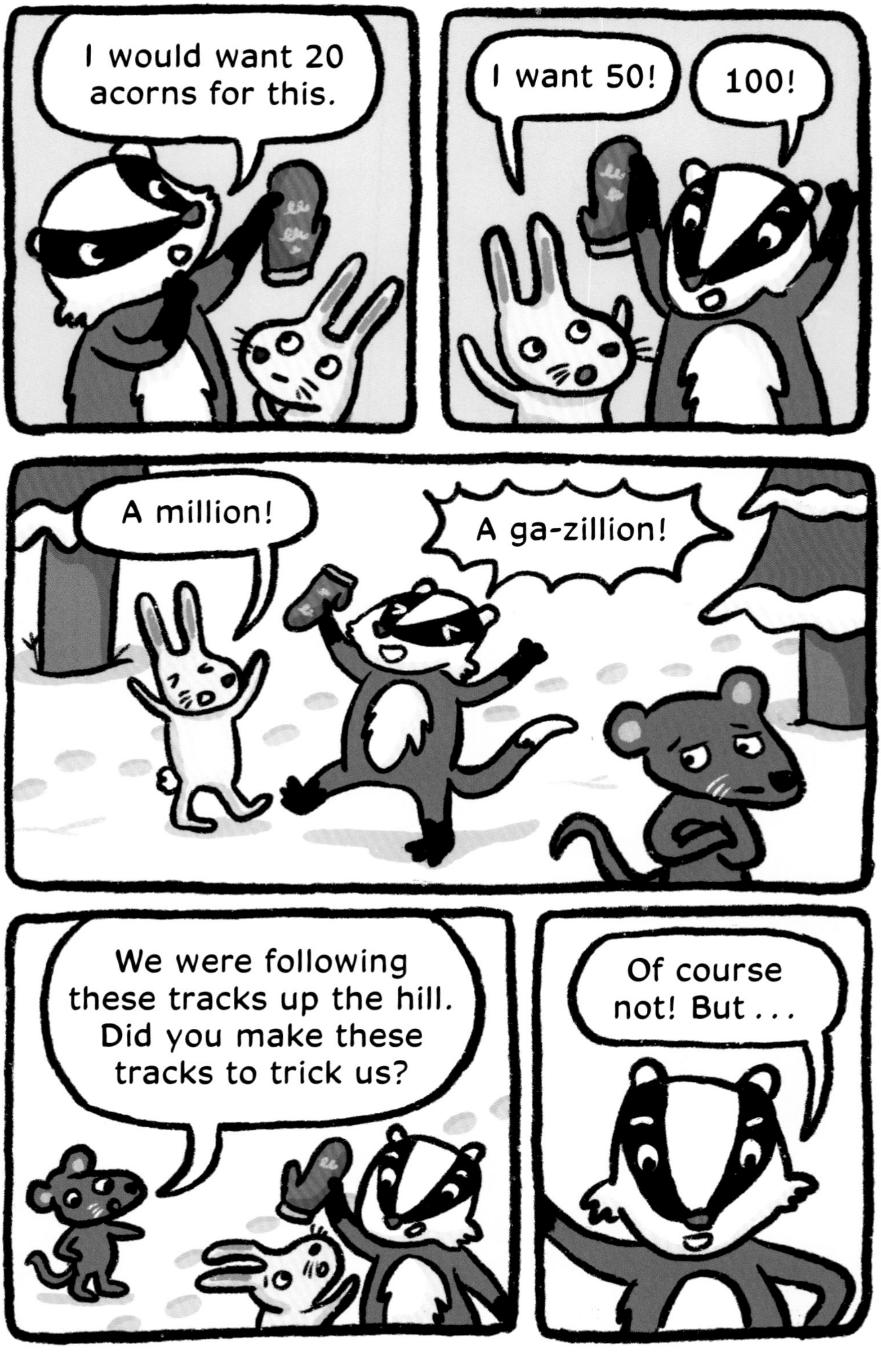
I would want 20 acorns for this.
I want 50!
100!
A million!
A ga-zillion!
We were following these tracks up the hill. Did you make these tracks to trick us?
Of course not! But . . .

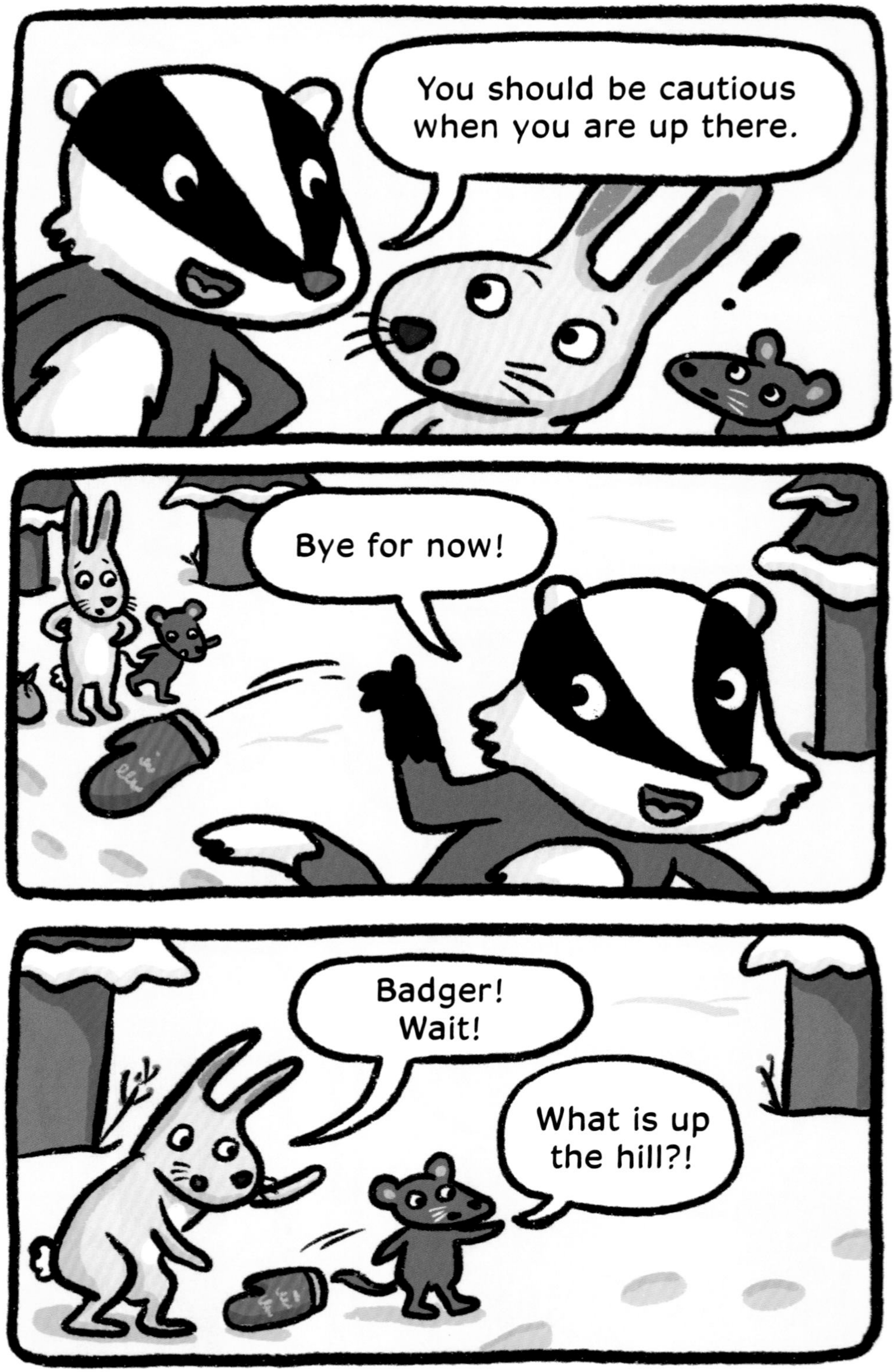
You should be cautious when you are up there.
Bye for now!
Badger! Wait!
What is up the hill?!

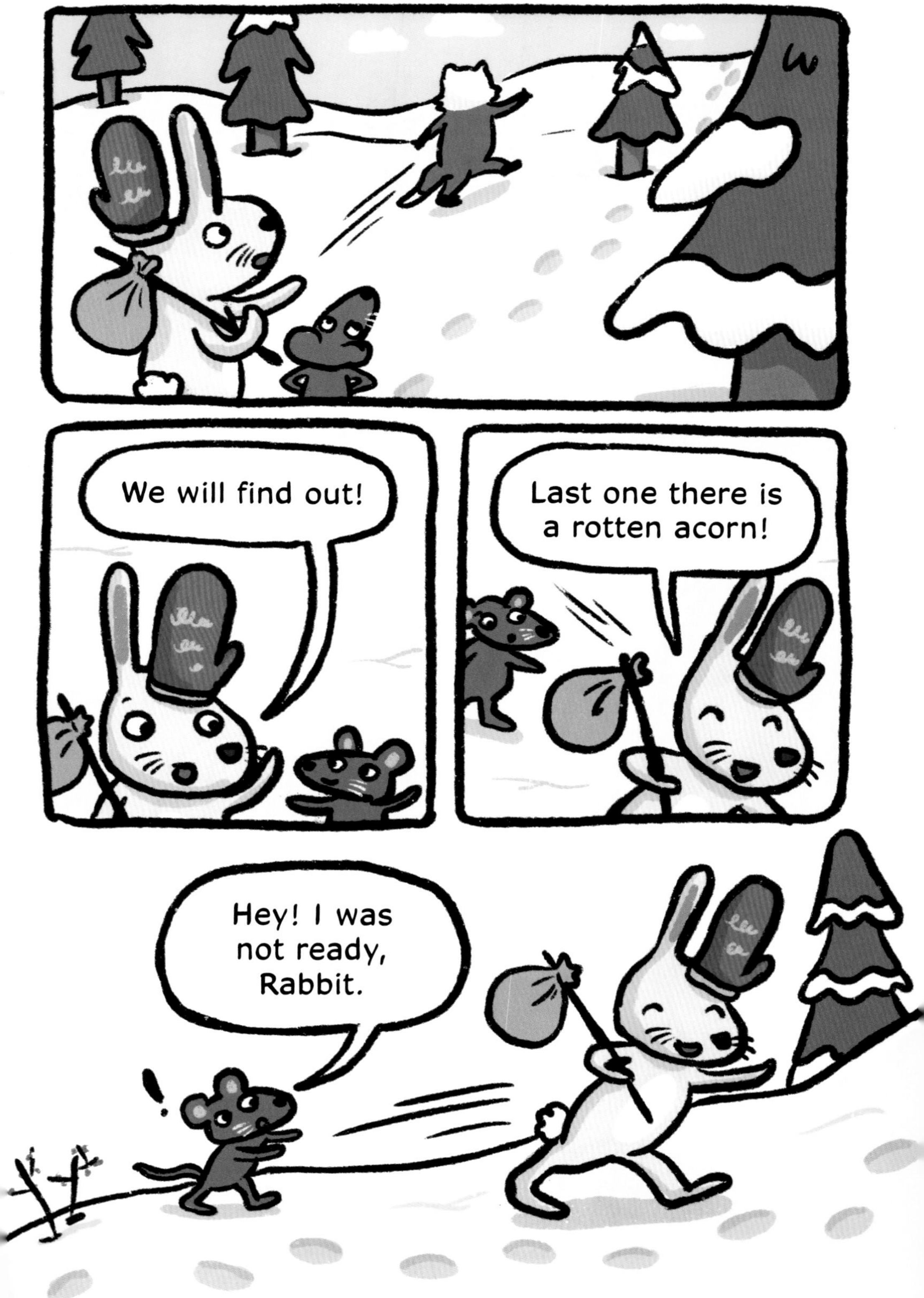
We will find out!
Last one there is a rotten acorn!
Hey! I was not ready, Rabbit.
!

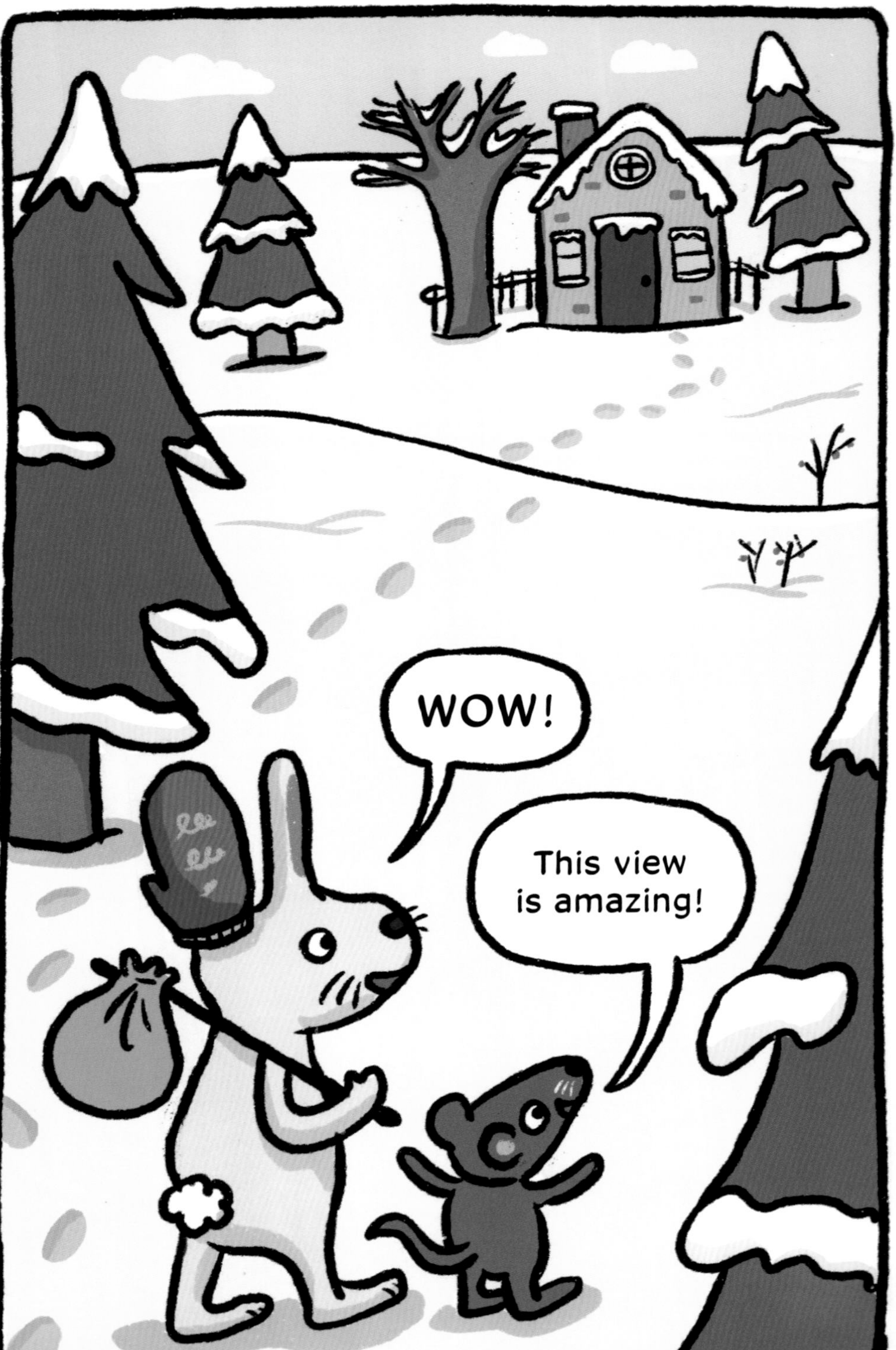
WOW!
This view is amazing!

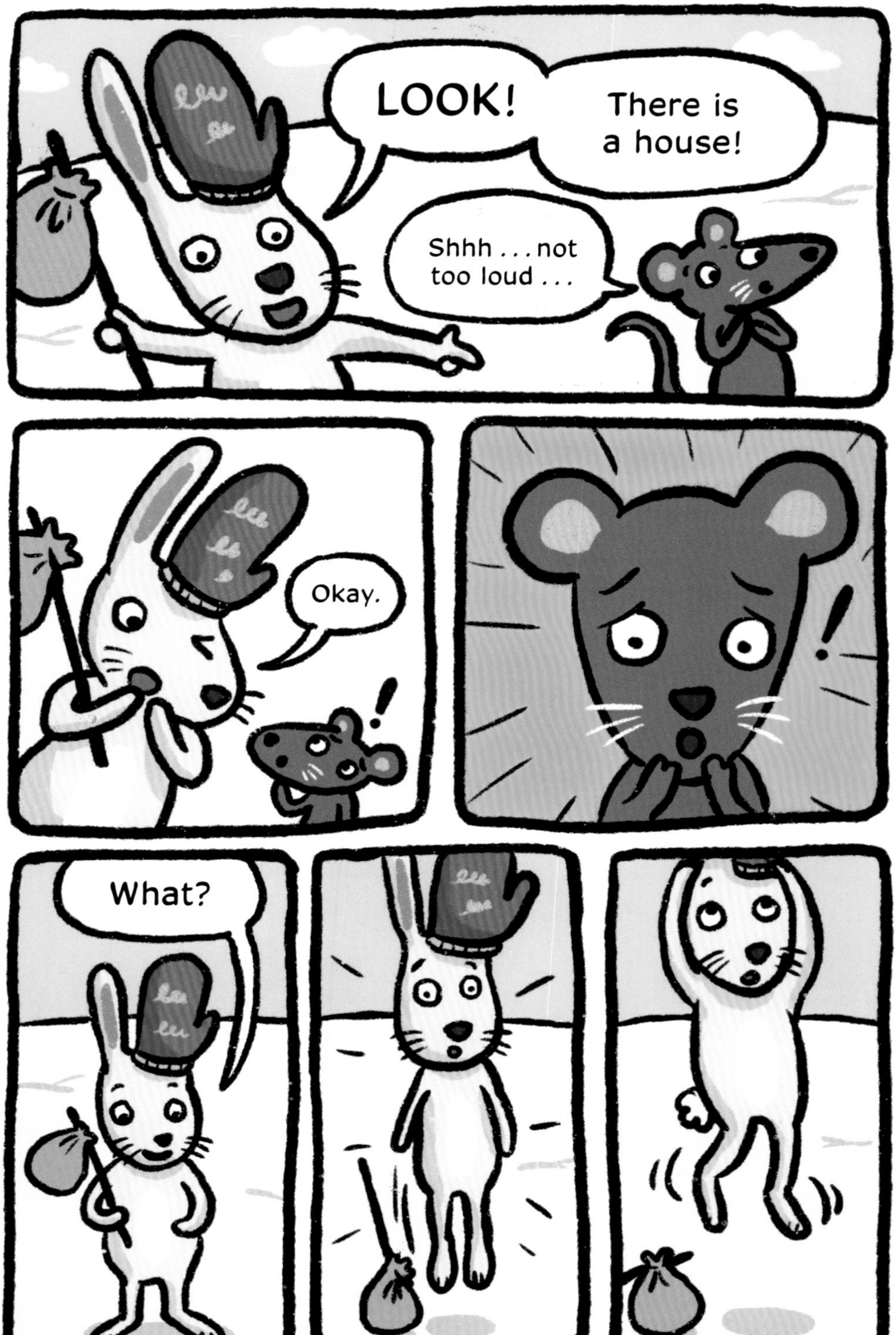
LOOK!
There is a house!
Shhh . . . not too loud . . .
Okay.
What?

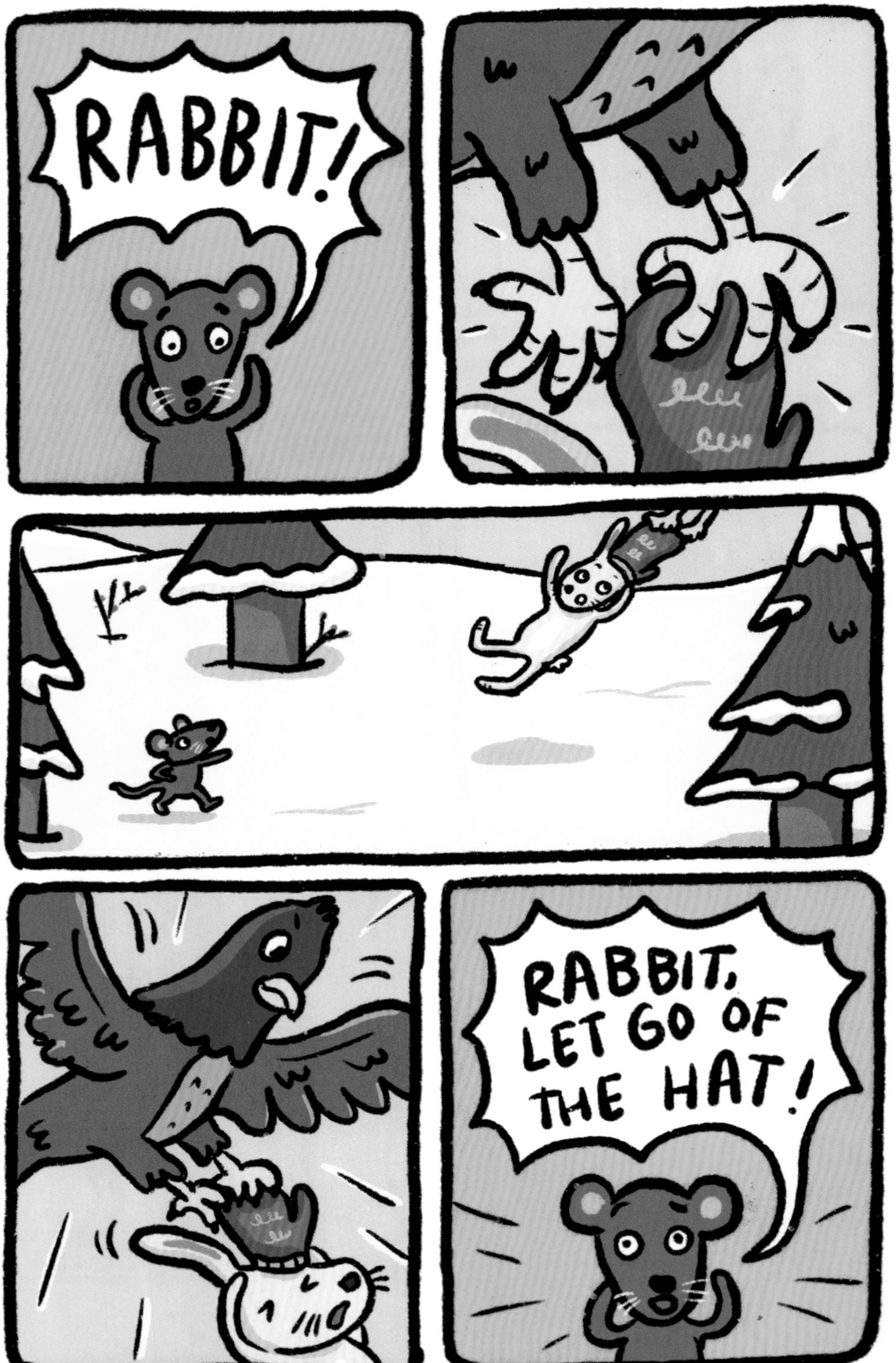
RABBIT!
RABBIT, LET GO OF THE HAT!

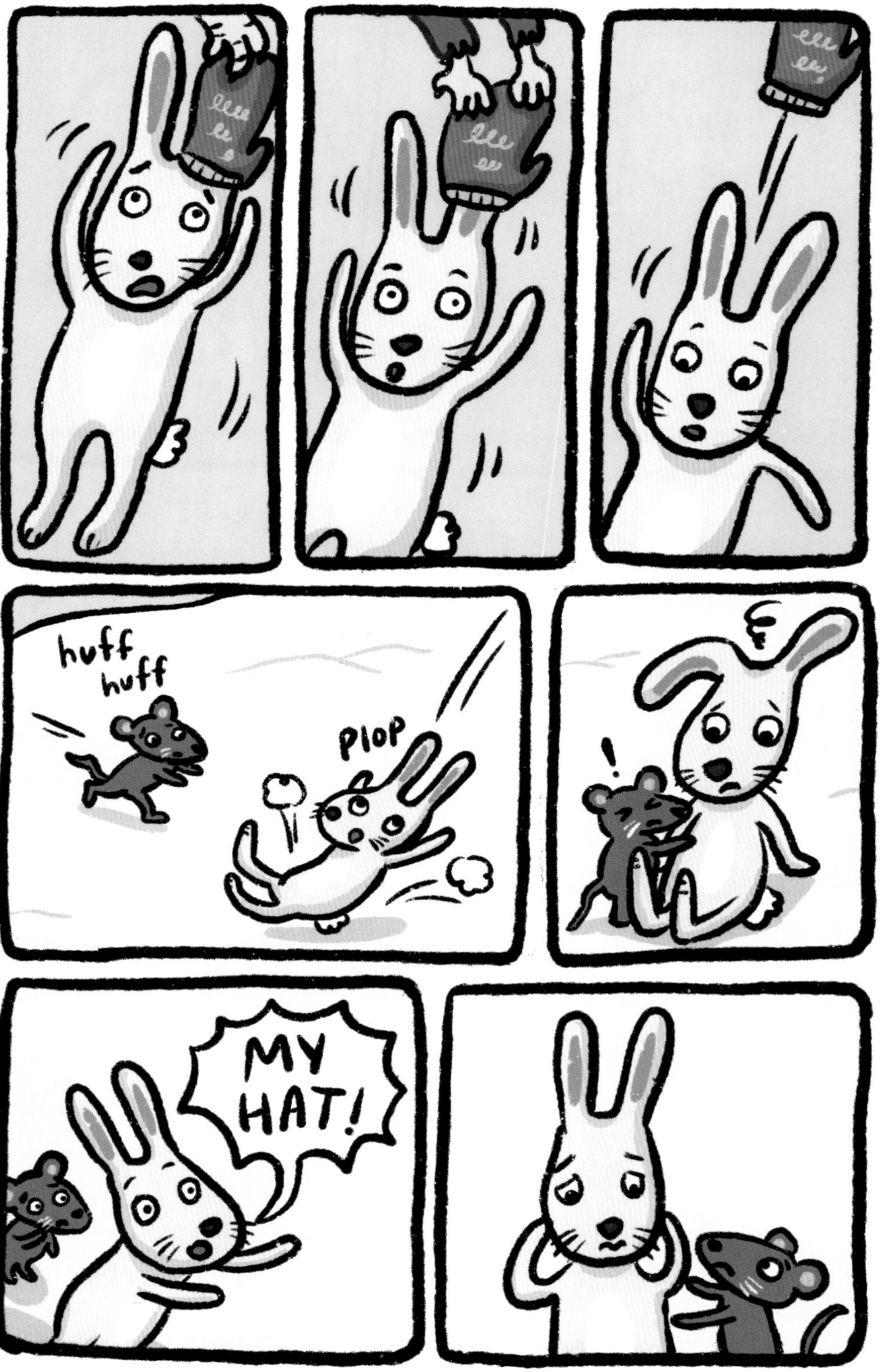
huff
huff
PLOP
!
MY HAT!

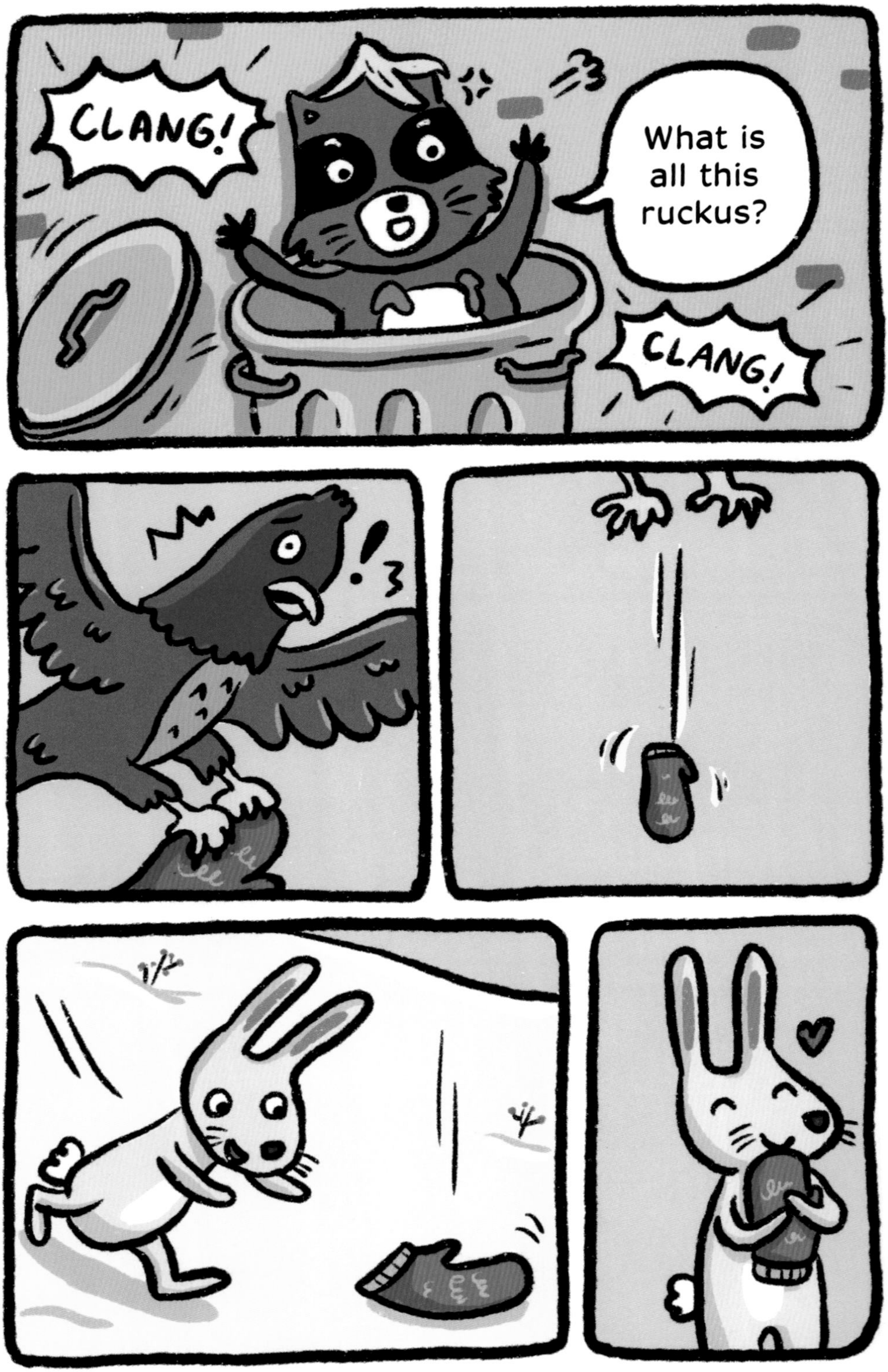
CLANG!
What is all this ruckus?
CLANG!

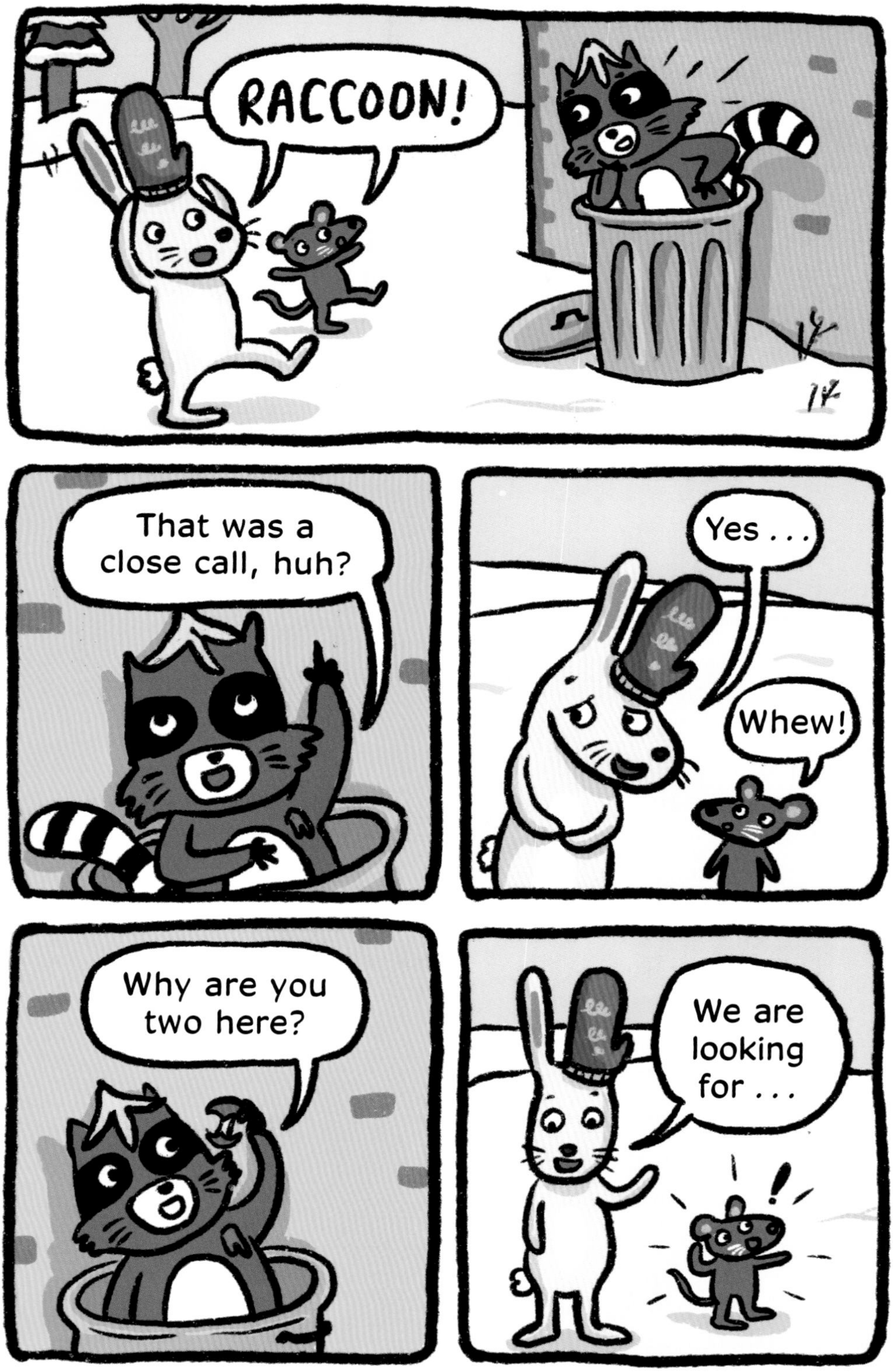
RACCOON!
That was a close call, huh?
Yes . . .
Whew!
Why are you two here?
We are looking for . . .

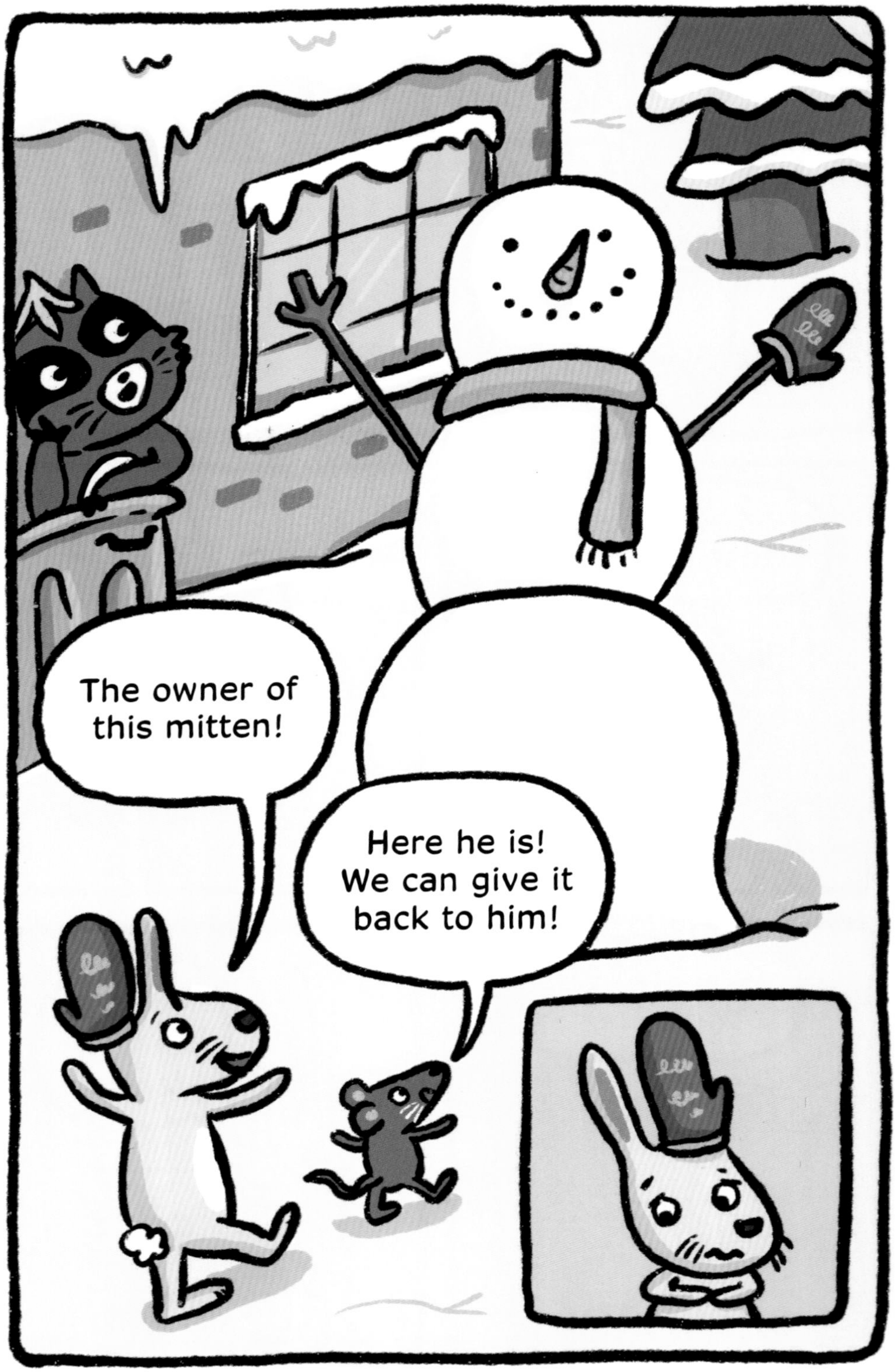
The owner of this mitten!
Here he is! We can give it back to him!

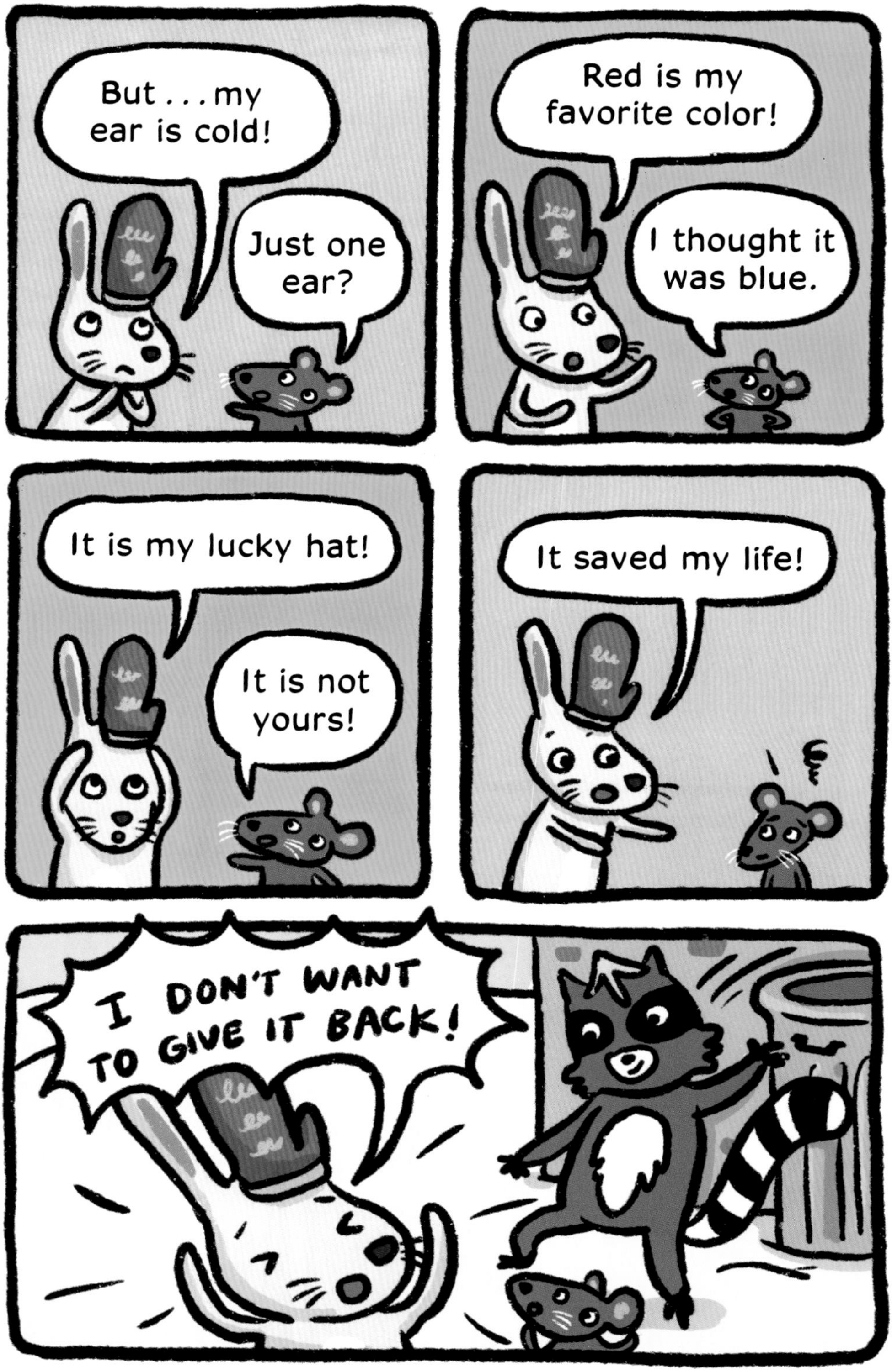

But . . . my ear is cold!
Just one ear?
Red is my favorite color!
I thought it was blue.
It is my lucky hat!
It is not yours!
It saved my life!
I DON'T WANT TO GIVE IT BACK!

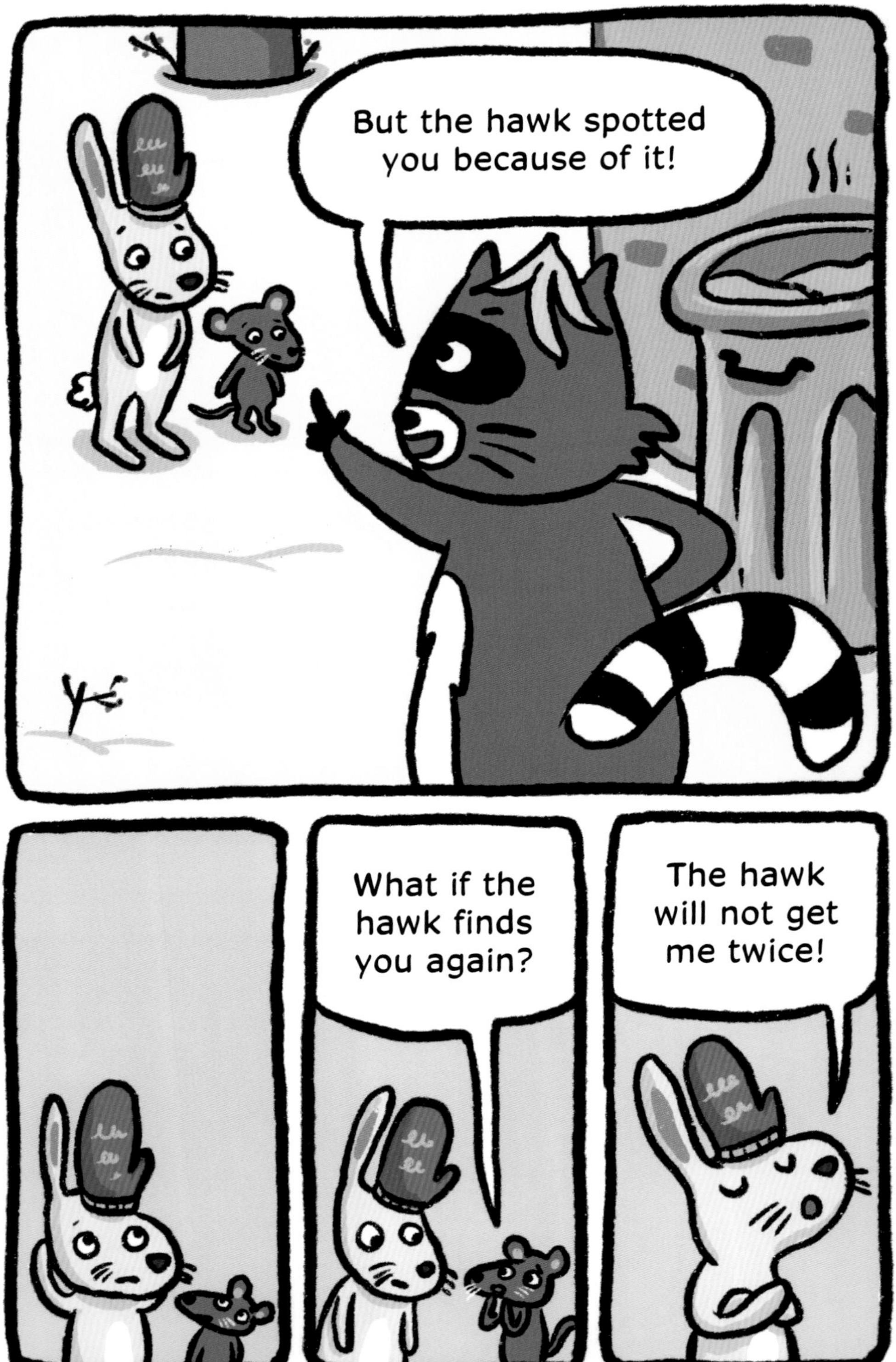
But the hawk spotted you because of it!
What if the hawk finds you again?
The hawk will not get me twice!

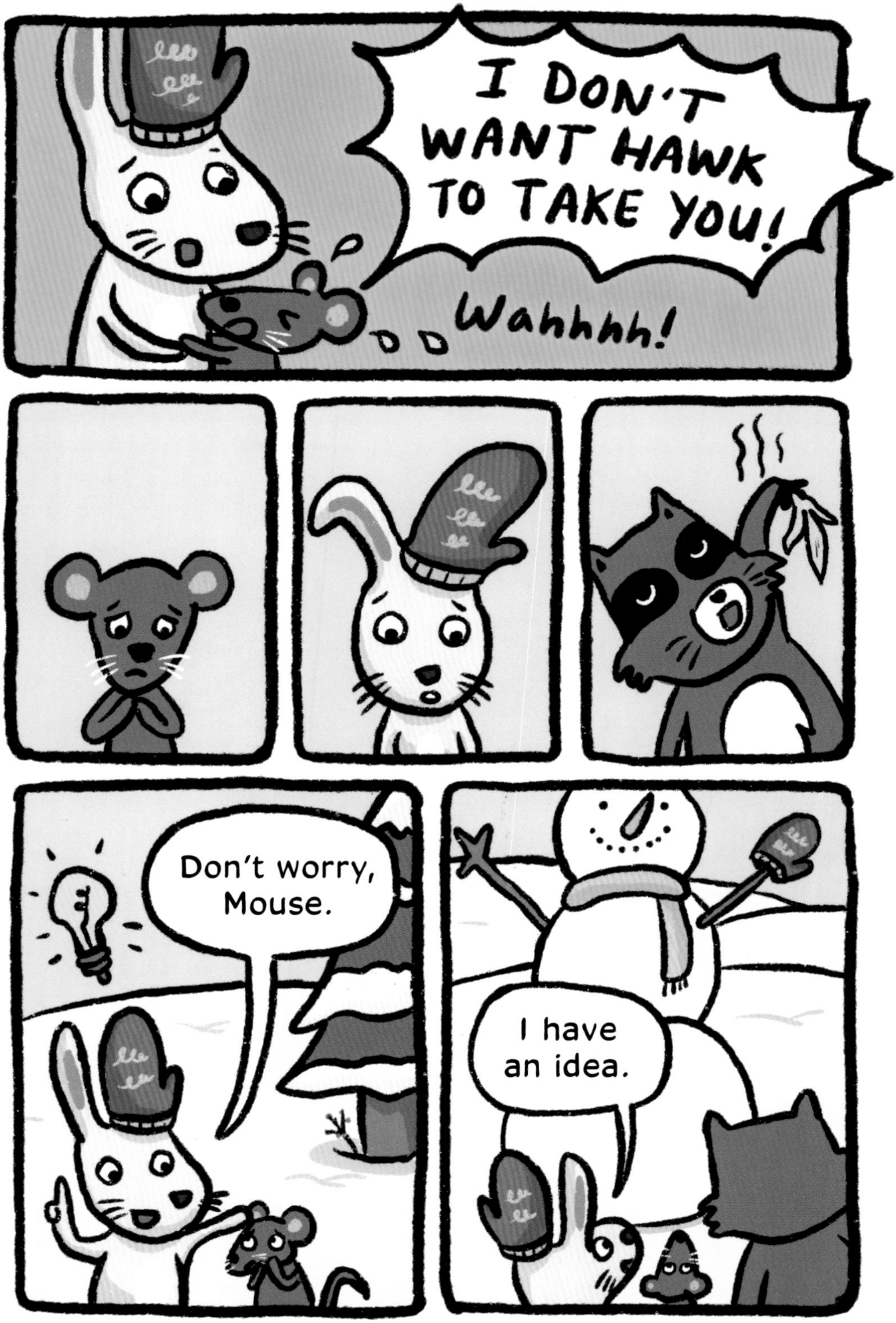
I DON'T WANT HAWK TO TAKE YOU!
Wahhhh!
Don't worry, Mouse.
I have an idea.

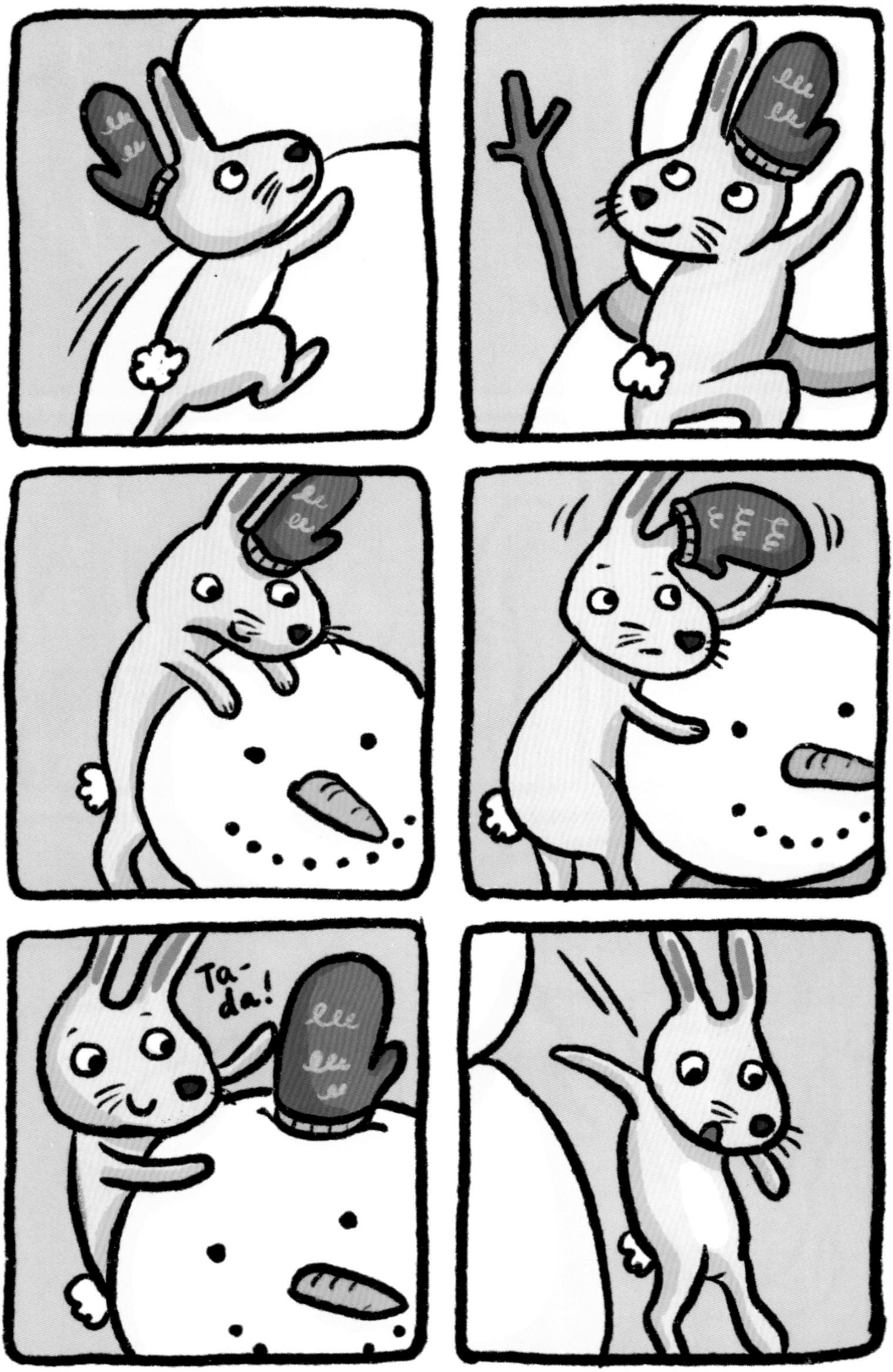
Ta-da!

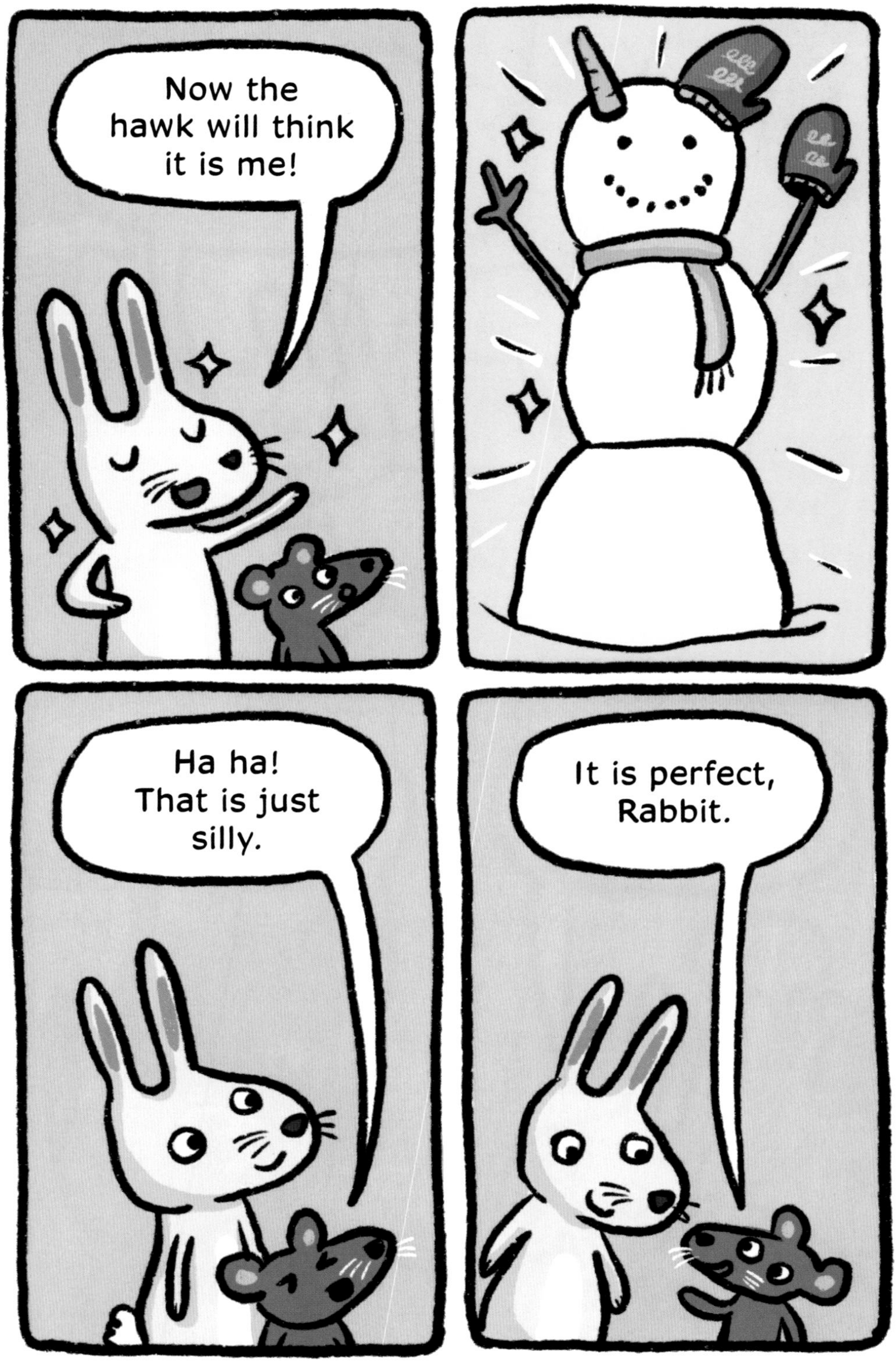
Now the hawk will think it is me!
Ha ha! That is just silly.
It is perfect, Rabbit.

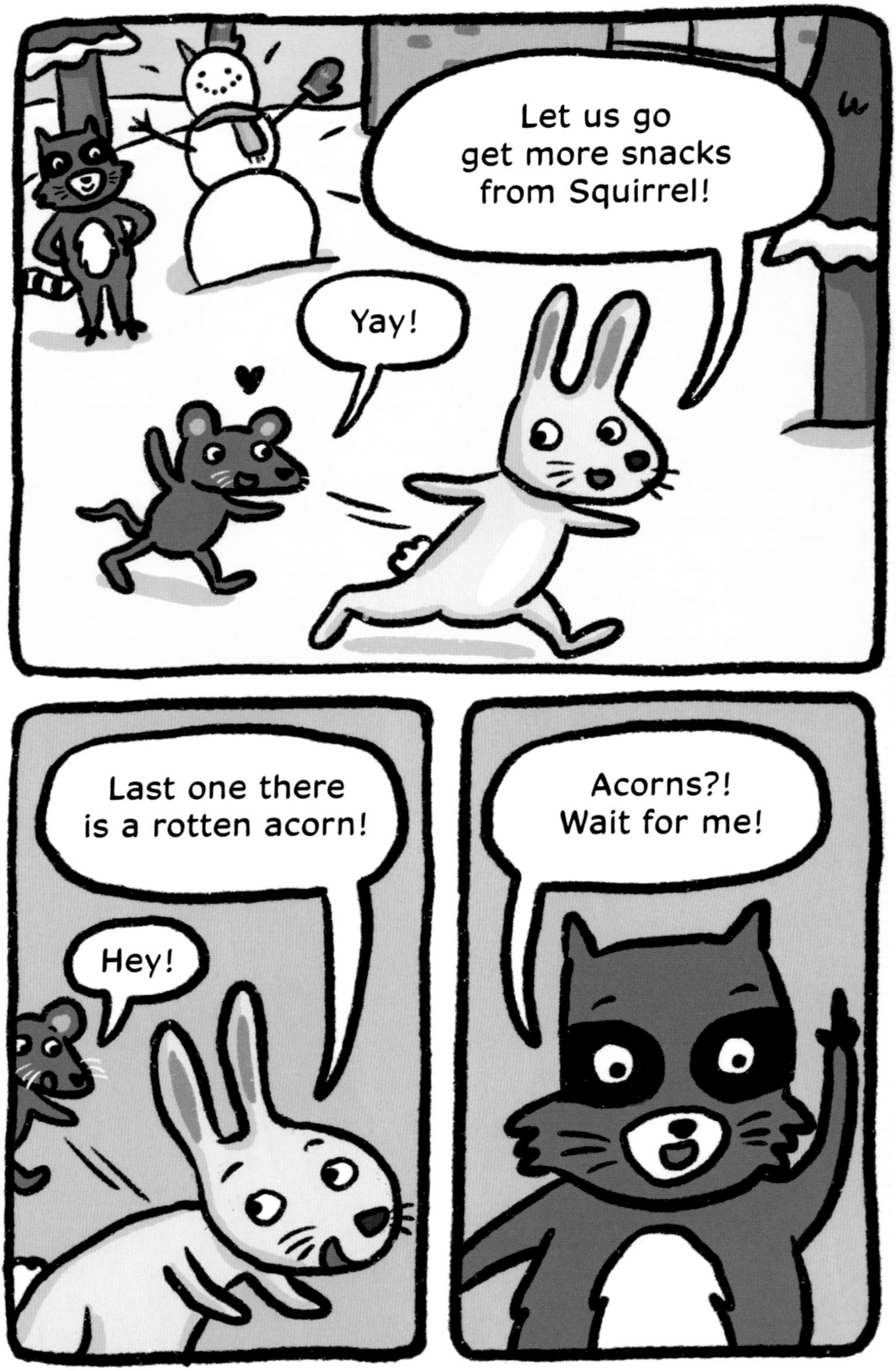
Let us go get more snacks from Squirrel!
Yay!
Last one there is a rotten acorn!
Hey!
Acorns?! Wait for me!

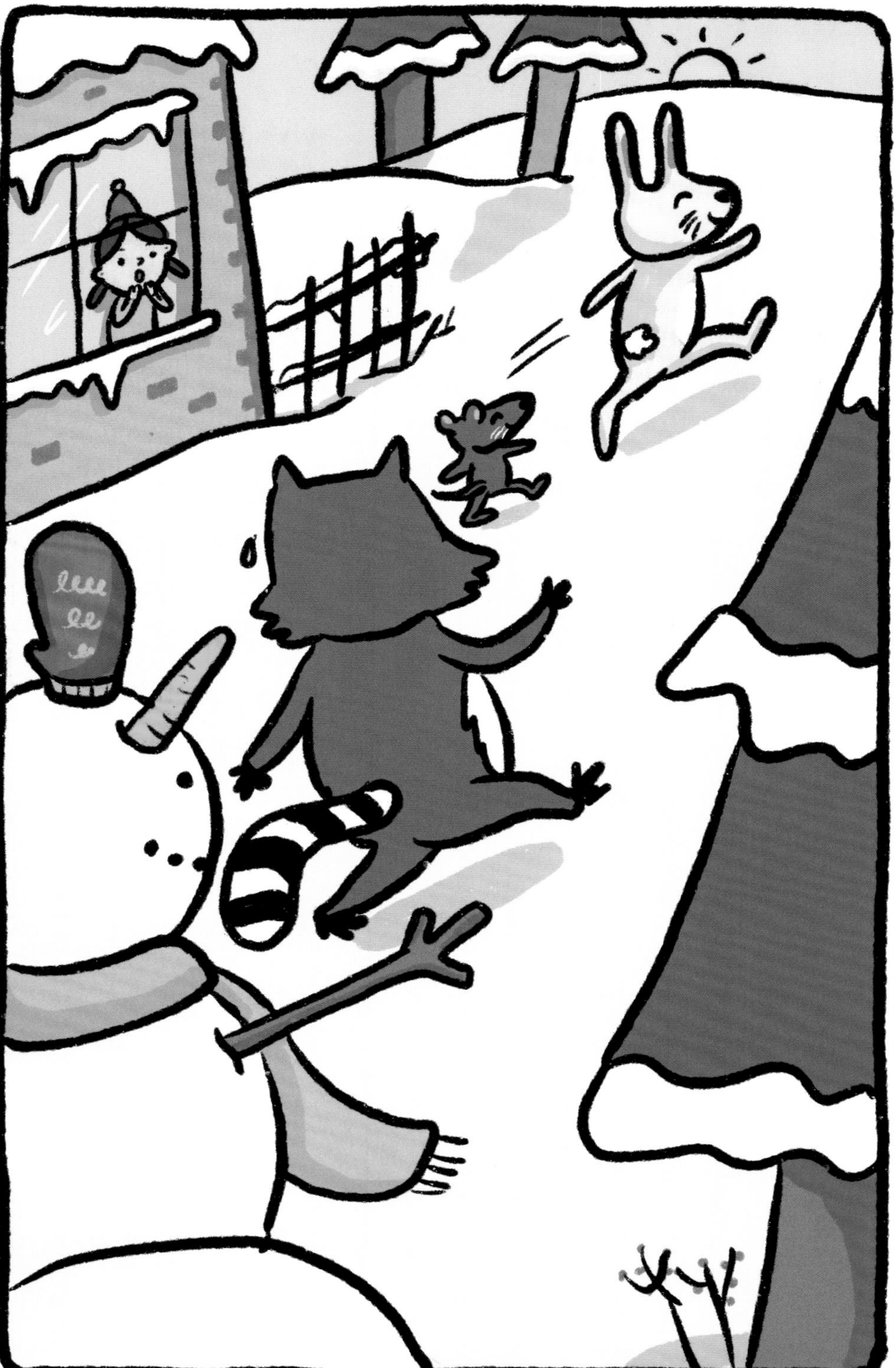

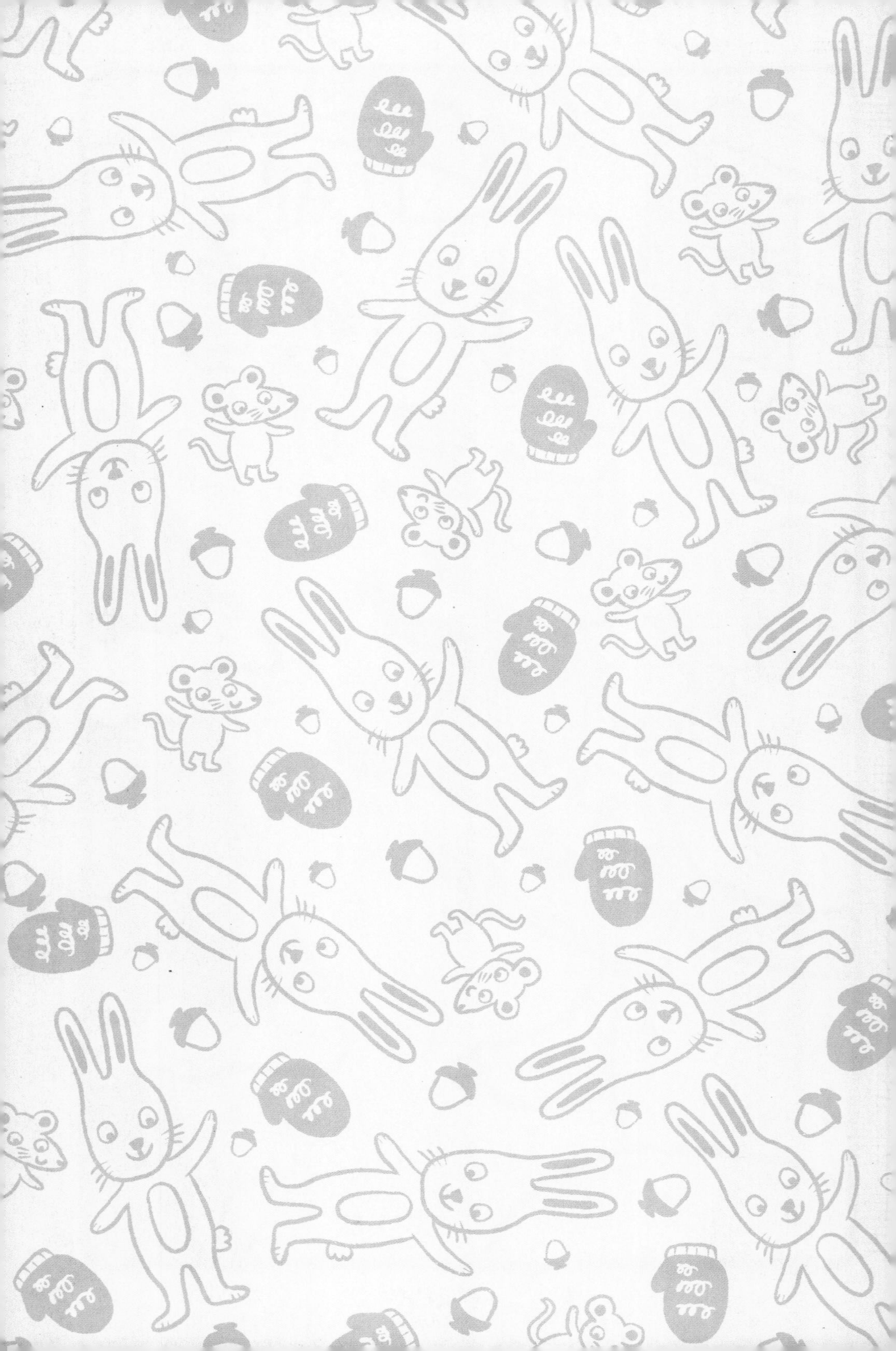